United States Presidents

ULYSSES S. GRANT

Series Consultant:
*Don M. Coerver, professor of history
Texas Christian University, Fort Worth, Texas*

Michael A. Schuman

 **Enslow Publishers, Inc.**
40 Industrial Road   PO Box 38
Box 398   Aldershot
Berkeley Heights, NJ 07922   Hants GU12 6BP
USA   UK
http://www.enslow.com

To Harold and Bernice Jensen, two loving grandparents.

Copyright © 2004 by Michael A. Schuman

All rights reserved.

No part of this book may be reproduced by any means without the written permission of the publisher.

Library of Congress Cataloging-in-Publication Data

Schuman, Michael.
　　Ulysses S. Grant / Michael A. Schuman.
　　　p. cm. — (United States presidents)
　　Summary: Examines the life and times of the eighteenth president of the United States, discussing his personal life as well as his military and political careers.
　　Includes bibliographical references (p.　) and index.
　　ISBN 0-7660-2038-X
　　1. Grant, Ulysses S. (Ulysses Simpson), 1822–1885—Juvenile literature.
2. Presidents—United States—Biography—Juvenile literature. [1. Grant, Ulysses S. (Ulysses Simpson), 1822–1885. 2. Presidents.] I. Title. II. Series.
　　E672.S38　2004
　　973.8'2'092—dc22

2003015641

Printed in the United States of America

10 9 8 7 6 5 4 3 2 1

To Our Readers:
We have done our best to make sure all Internet Addresses in this book were active and appropriate when we went to press. However, the author and the publisher have no control over and assume no liability for the material available on those Internet sites or on other Web sites they may link to. Any comments or suggestions can be sent by e-mail to comments@enslow.com or to the address on the back cover.

Illustration Credits: © 1996-2003 ArtToday.com, Inc., pp. 6 (top and bottom), 8, 28, 37, 48 (left and right), 49, 67, 72, 95; Enslow Publishers, Inc., p. 39; Courtesy of the Galena Historical Society, p. 33; Library of Congress, pp. 89, 104; Courtesy of the Ohio Historical Society Archives/Library, pp. 14, 21; Michael A. Schuman, pp. 11, 12, 16, 31, 52 (top and bottom), 103, 106.

Source Document Credits: Library of Congress, pp. 41, 45, 46, 59, 61, 63, 77, 81, 85, 98, 102, 109.

Cover Illustration: White House Collection, Courtesy White House Historical Association.

Contents

    Acknowledgments 4
1 Through Mud and Muck 5
2 The Tanner's Son 10
3 Crossing the Creek 20
4 "He *Fights*" 35
5 "Let Us Have Peace" 47
6 No King Midas 58
7 A Victory, a Panic, and a Wedding . . . 70
8 "One Honest Man in St. Louis" 83
9 ". . . How I Can Ever Trust Any Human Being Again" 93
10 Legacy 107
    "Death of General Grant" 112
    Chronology 113
    Did You Know? 116
    Chapter Notes 117
    Further Reading 122
    Internet Addresses 123
    Places to Visit 124
    Index 127

Acknowledgments

I wish to offer many thanks to those who kindly shared with me their time and expertise: Pam Sanfilippo, Judy Ruthven, Dr. Stephen Grove, Jim Small, Professor John Y. Simon, the staffs at the Keene Public and Keene State College libraries, and my children Trisha and Ally, who must have thought this book was another sibling.

1

Through Mud and Muck

General Ulysses S. Grant tramped alongside his troops, marching through the swamps and forests of the mid-South. It was 1863, in the middle of the Civil War.

A total of eleven Southern states had seceded from the United States just two years earlier. They formed their own separate nation, the Confederate States of America. The North and South had had disputes over several issues that led to the war, including slavery, trade, and states' rights. Now the North, or the Union, was battling to keep the Southern states a part of the nation. It was not easy.

Grant, a Union general, was aware that the Union campaign had become bogged down in the state of Mississippi, on the east side of the Mississippi River.

Ulysses S. Grant

Left: Ulysses S. Grant, a Union general during the Civil War, knew he was about to fight in a key battle at Vicksburg in Mississippi. **Below:** To help Grant seize Vicksburg, gunboats and other ships surrounded the town from the water.

Through Mud and Muck

He knew that if the Union could control the wide river, it would cut the Confederacy in two. It became apparent that the key to victory was the city of Vicksburg, Mississippi, which sat on a two hundred-foot-high bluff overlooking the river.

For about ten weeks, Grant's army tried to seize Vicksburg with no luck. Newspapers covering the war for the North called Grant lazy and stupid. But in the spring of 1863, Grant came up with a clever idea. He crossed the river with his forces and marched south along the river's west bank in Louisiana, opposite Vicksburg. For weeks they slogged through mud and muck. They trekked through swamps where alligators and poisonous snakes make their homes. Finally, when south of Vicksburg, they crossed the river again and began marching north to approach that vital town.

Unlike some generals, Grant stayed with his troops. He rode on his horse alongside them as they trudged 180 miles north over the course of three weeks. During that time, they fought five battles in five different towns. On May 19, they tried to take Vicksburg by force but were beaten back. Grant then did the only wise thing he could. He settled his troops in for a siege. They surrounded Vicksburg, battering it with their guns. Below, on the Mississippi River, Union admiral David Porter bombarded the stately town from gunboats.

The people of Vicksburg became desperate. Their food supply ran so low they resorted to eating dogs, horses, and mules. Finally, on July 4, 1863, the

Ulysses S. Grant

Confederates surrendered. Grant and the Union now had control of the Mississippi including the major port of New Orleans. The Union officers held a celebration that evening aboard one of Admiral Porter's boats.

Among his fellow officers, Grant commonly stood out like a wart. He was hardly a typical general. He was not a tall, commanding figure who stood erect and beamed in a sparkling uniform. Grant was stocky and unkempt. By 1863, he had a scruffy black beard with a tinge of gray. His height has been listed in different historical accounts as anywhere between five foot seven inches and five foot nine inches tall. He walked

In July 1863, the Confederates surrendered. Grant and the Union had control over the Mississippi River.

stooped over, which made him appear even shorter than he was.

In addition, Grant never cared for military traditions, such as marching bands or parades in uniform. He hated the sight of blood, although critics have said an injured human did not bother him as much as an injured horse. Once during the war, he lost his temper when he saw a man beating a horse on the head. Grant grabbed the man by the throat and ordered that he be tied to a post for six hours as punishment.

Grant was truly an uncommon war hero, who would become an uncommon president.

The Tanner's Son

Ulysses S. Grant was born in a three-room cabin on April 27, 1822, in Point Pleasant, Ohio, a small town about twenty miles southeast of Cincinnati in the southwestern corner of the state. The birthplace sits on a bluff overlooking the Ohio River. Standing outside the little white cabin, one can easily see the state of Kentucky on the other side of the water.

When one says the word "frontier" today, people might think of the Great Plains of Nebraska or perhaps the desert of Arizona. However, when Ulysses S. Grant was a baby, this part of Ohio was very much the frontier of the United States. Ohio had been a state for only nineteen years, and Point Pleasant was sparsely settled. There were fewer than twelve homes in the village.[1]

Grant's father, Jesse, worked in a tannery next to the

The Tanner's Son

This cozy cabin was the birthplace of the future president.

house, which his wife, Hannah Simpson Grant, cared for. Tanners prepare animal hides to be used as clothing or upholstery. The job was not one for a person with a weak stomach. Animals kept in a tanyard were slaughtered, usually in great pain. The hides were often caked with blood, hair, or pieces of skin when brought to the tannery. The tanner stored the hides in salt to preserve them, then soaked them in lye so the hair would fall off. Then they were put in tubs of tannic acid to become flexible and strong. The smell coming from an active tannery can be sickening to some people.

Ulysses was Jesse and Hannah Grant's first child. He was a big baby, weighing almost eleven pounds at birth.

He had blue eyes, a light complexion, and reddish-brown hair. One thing he did not have for nearly a month was a name. Hannah wanted to name him Albert, in honor of an American diplomat named Albert Gallatin. Her father liked the name Hiram, while her mother favored Ulysses, after a hero in Greek mythology.

It was decided to write all the names on pieces of paper and place them in a hat. Hannah's sister Anne Simpson drew the name Ulysses from the hat. However, Jesse decided a compromise was in order. To keep both his mother-in-law and father-in-law happy, he decided to name the baby Hiram Ulysses Grant. His parents called him Ulysses, or Lyss, for short.

When Lyss was just a year and a half old, his father

The Grant family moved from Point Pleasant, Ohio, to this home in Georgetown, Ohio, in 1824.

moved the family twenty miles east to Georgetown, Ohio. Georgetown was not much bigger than Point Pleasant, but the area had more natural resources. The gushing White Oak River, a tributary of the Ohio, flowed through town. Also close by were soaring stands of hardwood forest. Running water and tanbark, or bark of specific trees used as a source of tannic acid, were essential for the tanning trade.

The Grants moved into a handsome brick two-story home near the center of town. It was no mansion, but it was an impressive sight in Georgetown at the time. National Park Service historian Pam Sanfilippo said, "Most biographies say that Grant came from a poor frontier background. That's not really true. Jesse Grant was fairly well to do for his time. He built the first brick home in Georgetown. He was a pretty shrewd businessman and had political connections."[2]

Sanfilippo added that Jesse Grant spared nothing when it came to his son. She noted, "Since Jesse was self-educated, he was insistent on his son getting a good education. Grant's education was one of the best that could have been received by any child for that area in that time."[3]

There were no public schools in that area, so Grant attended a subscription school. Instead of paying taxes, parents paid the tuition for their children's educations. There was usually one teacher and thirty or forty students in a classroom. They could range in age from three to twenty years old.

Ulysses S. Grant

Lyss Grant was an average student. The only subject he truly enjoyed was arithmetic. In the classroom he was shy. One girl remembered him as "a real nice boy who never had anything to say, and when he said anything, he always said it short."[4]

Outside school, Grant liked to play ball or swim in a nearby creek in summer. In winter, he would skate or go on sleigh rides. Grant's father remembered how Lyss enjoyed marbles. Most of all, he loved horses. At five years old, Lyss could stand on the back of a trotting horse. By the time he was seven, the boy was able to harness a horse to haul wood. People in Georgetown

Ulysses S. Grant, as a child, worked in his father's tannery.

The Tanner's Son

were amazed at his ability. Anyone in town who had trouble training a horse would bring it to Lyss Grant, who seemed to work magic with the animals.

One time Grant's desire to own a colt led to an embarrassing incident. A man named Mr. Ralston wanted to sell the colt for twenty-five dollars. But Grant's father told him it was worth only twenty dollars, and he wanted his son to bargain with Mr. Ralston. So Grant said to Mr. Ralston, "Papa says I may offer you twenty dollars for the colt, but if you won't take that, I am to offer you twenty-two and a half, and if you won't take that, to give you twenty-five."[5]

Of course, Mr. Ralston got the full price, twenty-five dollars. Grant was teased about his foolish transaction. He later confessed, "The story got out among the boys of the village, and it was a long time before I heard the last of it. Boys enjoy the misery of their companions, at least village boys in that day did."[6]

Grant later defended himself, saying, "I certainly showed very plainly that I had come for the colt and meant to have him."[7] Most of the people in Georgetown, however, saw Grant's actions as those of a senseless boy.

The horse bargaining adventure was doubly embarrassing because Jesse Grant constantly boasted about his young son. Judy Ruthven, chairman of the U.S. Grant Homestead Foundation in Georgetown, Ohio, said, "Jesse Grant had no doubt that his son would be great. Ulysses was very quiet and reserved as a boy. He was attractive and well thought of, but his father bragged about him so much that he took a lot of teasing for that from the people in town and from his classmates."[8] Because he could not live up to his father's expectations, Grant was given an unkind nickname by residents of Georgetown: "Useless Grant."

As Lyss got older, the Grant family expanded. Jesse and Hannah had five more children. As the oldest, Lyss was allowed to move into a room on the second floor of their Georgetown home. The problem with his new room was that it overlooked his father's smelly, dark tannery. Grant was sickened by the place and admitted he "detested" it.[9] He knew he never wanted to go into his father's business.

Jesse Grant wanted Ulysses to have a good education. One of the first schools he went to was this one in Georgetown, Ohio.

The Tanner's Son

Because Jesse Grant cared so much about his son's education, he sent Ulysses to private schools for two years as a teenager. Then, when Grant was seventeen, his father told him that he was going to attend the United States Military Academy at West Point, New York. Grant was not thrilled about the rigid lives West Point cadets are forced to lead. But Lyss's best subject was mathematics, and West Point was one of only two colleges in the country at the time that trained civil engineers.[10] Engineers need a strong background in math to succeed.

Grant had no interest in a military career, but an education at West Point is paid for by the federal government, with no charge to the student. Besides, it would allow him a chance to travel to another part of the United States.

Grant packed up his belongings as he prepared to leave for West Point in May 1839. But Grant cringed when he saw his initials, H.U.G., spelled out in brass tacks on his trunk. Having initials that spelled the word "hug" could be as humiliating as being called "Useless." From then on, he decided, he would be known as Ulysses Hiram Grant.

Upon arriving at West Point, Grant discovered that his name was listed incorrectly as Ulysses S. Grant. Senator Thomas Hamer, who had sponsored Grant, mistakenly believed Grant's middle name was Simpson, his mother's maiden name. So Grant had yet another name change, and became U. S. Grant. Because of these initials, fellow cadets began calling him "Uncle Sam." In time, he became known simply as Sam Grant.

At the time he entered West Point, Grant was a small, slight boy who stood only five feet one inch tall. He was surprised to find that he actually liked the academy. In a letter to a cousin named R. McKinstry Griffith dated September 22, 1839, Grant wrote that his new home was "decidedly the most beautiful place that I have ever seen," and "it seems as though I could live here ferever [sic] if my friends would only come too."[11]

Those feelings would not last. Grant soon became tired of military routines such as field exercises. He did well in subjects he found easy, such as mathematics, and nearly gave up in those that were difficult, including French. He showed talent at drawing, but suffered through a class called ethics, a combination of various subjects including grammar and geography. He naturally excelled in horsemanship.

Grant also piled up demerits, or marks against his record for misconduct. Most were not for serious violations, but for being sloppy or lazy. These demerits included not having his coat buttoned, not brushing his clothes, or oversleeping.

By the time Grant graduated in 1843, he had grown to five foot seven inches tall and had earned the rank of second lieutenant. In school, his final ranking placed him twenty-first out of thirty-nine cadets. He had also collected a total of 290 demerits, putting him in the middle of the average category.[12] Dr. Stephen Grove, a

The Tanner's Son

historian at West Point, said, "Motivation for anyone means a lot, and he simply wasn't interested."[13]

When Grant got his smart new uniform, he rode to Cincinnati. He wanted to show off to his former classmates, especially the girls. But as he rode into town on his horse, dressed splendidly in his army uniform, a poor barefooted boy in dirty and ragged clothes mocked him, saying, "Soldier! Will you work? No, sir-ee; I'll sell my shirt first."[14] A bit later Grant encountered a stable hand ridiculing the young West Point graduate by walking around wearing fake army uniform trousers.

Historian Pam Sanfilippo explained what the boy and stable hand meant. "There was no war going on, so soldiers were figureheads," she said. "Wearing an officer's uniform was a sign of the upper class. The boy meant that officers in the military think they are hot stuff but they are living off our taxes and don't work for a living. They don't get their hands dirty. Their nails are clean. The taunting brought him [Grant] to reality that the uniform doesn't make the man."[15]

As an adult, Grant wrote that the incidents, "gave me a distaste for military uniform that I never recovered from."[16]

3

CROSSING THE CREEK

After graduating from West Point, Grant was required to serve in the army for four years. That was how he would repay the government for his education. Following his four-year stint, Grant planned to quit the army and teach mathematics in college.

Second Lieutenant Grant was assigned to the 4th Infantry at Jefferson Barracks in St. Louis, Missouri. He reported for duty on September 30, 1843. St. Louis was a good match for Grant. One of his West Point roommates, Fred Dent, came from the area. Dent had grown up in a well-to-do family on a plantation named White Haven just ten miles from the barracks. Grant often rode a horse to visit the Dents at their plantation home.

Slavery was legal in Missouri, and the Dents owned

Crossing the Creek

After going to West Point, Grant was ready to serve in the army.

slaves. Grant did not approve of slavery, but he did not interfere with the Dents' way of life. However, he did become very close to the family. In February 1844, he met his roommate's seventeen-year-old sister, Julia, and he was soon spending more time with her than with Fred.

Julia was not pretty by most people's standards. She was about five feet tall and had a stocky build. She also suffered from a condition called strabismus, or weak eye muscles. Because of that, she could not control her right eye properly.

But Grant looked beyond her physical features. He found her intelligent and fun to talk with. She shared his love of horses and enjoyed other outdoor activities such as fishing. Back then it was not considered appropriate for a girl to fish, so to appear more feminine, Julia asked a brother or a slave to bait her hook for her.

Grant cared about her and did special things to show it. When Julia's pet canary died, Grant crafted a little yellow coffin and conducted a funeral for the bird. He even brought eight of his fellow officers along to attend the ceremony.

In April 1844, Grant received word that he would be transferred to Camp Salubrity, an army base in Louisiana. Before he left, he asked Julia if she would wear his class ring. At the time, it was the closest thing to being engaged. Julia liked Grant but was not ready to commit herself to him. They had known each other only two months.

Crossing the Creek

Before moving, Grant was given some leave, or time off. He visited his family in Ohio, then returned to St. Louis to see Julia one more time. But his visit was not going to be easy.

In front of White Haven is Gravois Creek, which must be crossed to reach the house. It usually is very shallow, except during heavy rains, which happened to be the case on the day Grant visited. The creek was overflowing.

National Park Service historian Pam Sanfilippo explained, "Grant had a personal motto—some call it a superstition—that he wouldn't retrace his steps. He realized someone was at White Haven who meant quite a lot to him. So he rode his horse into the creek and was nearly swept away. He came out okay, but was soaking wet. He borrowed some dry clothes from Julia's brother, who was a lot taller. The clothes didn't fit, but he proposed [marriage] anyway."[1]

That incident became a symbol of Grant's determined nature. When he wanted something, he would let nothing stand in his way.

Grant again asked Julia to marry him. This time she said yes. According to Sanfilippo, she probably agreed because she had known him longer, and she was aware that he was going away. But there was a problem. Julia knew her father, Colonel Frederick Dent, would object. Colonel Dent did not think an army officer could ever make enough money to keep his daughter happy. It was important in that day for a father to give permission for his daughter to be married. Julia and Grant decided to keep their engagement secret for the time being.

Grant arrived at Camp Salubrity in June 1844. Without Julia nearby, he was bored and passed time betting on horse races or playing cards with other soldiers. But his mind was always on his fiancée. They wrote letters, but Grant was often frustrated since he wrote more often than she replied. In one letter in September 1844, he complained, "It has only been a few days since I received your letters. I answered them immediately, won't you be as punctual in answering mine in the future? You don't know Julia with how much anxiety and suspense I await there [sic] arrival."[2]

Julia tried to convince her father to allow her to marry Grant. He responded, "You are too young and the boy is too poor. He hasn't anything to give you."[3]

In April 1845, Grant was given another leave. He traveled to St. Louis to try to convince Julia's father to allow him to marry his daughter. Grant admitted that the army was not his career goal. He wanted to be a mathematics professor. Dent gave Grant formal permission to continue dating Julia, but not to marry her.

Grant soon had more on his mind than his engagement. Far south of Missouri, trouble was brewing. Mexico and the United States had had disagreements for years. Much of the bad blood between the two nations concerned Texas. Mexico had controlled Texas from 1820 until Texas revolted in 1835. In 1836, Texas declared itself an independent republic. However,

Crossing the Creek

Mexico never recognized Texas's independence. Mexico warned that should the United States admit Texas to the Union, Mexico would cut off all diplomatic relations with the United States. When Texas became a state in 1845, the government of Mexico did just that.

This crisis might have been settled peacefully, but there were more disputes, one of which was over land. The United States claimed its border with Mexico was the Rio Grande River. Mexico disagreed and said the border between the two countries was the Nueces River, farther north. In addition, the United States claimed that Mexico owed about $3 million to American citizens stemming from American lives and land lost during Mexico's war with Spain over twenty years earlier.

In the early spring of 1846, the Americans under General Zachary Taylor established a camp on the north bank of the Rio Grande. Mexican general Pedro de Ampudia gave an ultimatum to the Americans: Retreat to the Nueces River or a state of war will exist. Taylor replied that he had no authority to withdraw and stayed put.

A week later, the Mexican cavalry entered American soil upstream from Taylor's encampment. Men sent by Taylor to investigate the movement were ambushed and sixteen were either killed or wounded. When word of the attack got back to President James K. Polk, the chief executive asked Congress to declare war on Mexico. On May 13, 1846, Congress did so.

As an active member of the United States Army,

Grant knew he would be called to fight. He wrote to Julia, "Don't fear for me My Dear Julia for this is only the active part of our business. It is just what we come here for and the sooner it begins, the sooner it will end and probably be the means of my seeing my Dear Julia soon. You don't know how anxious I am to see you again Julia."[4]

But the war did not end soon, and Grant saw much action under General Zachary Taylor. In one of the war's first battles at Palo Alto, Mexico, Grant witnessed first-hand the horror of war. He wrote, "One cannon-ball passed through our ranks, not far from me. It took off the head of an enlisted man, and the under jaw of Captain Page of my regiment, while the splinters from the musket of the killed soldier, and his brains and bones, knocked down two or three others."[5]

The Americans won the battle at Palo Alto and a second smaller battle soon afterwards. They marched deeper into Mexico. Grant would soon play a bigger role in the war. Because of his mathematical ability and skill with horses, in August 1846, Grant was named quartermaster of the 4th Infantry. His job was to take care of supplies including money and transportation.

On September 23, 1846, Grant proved his courage. The Americans and Mexicans were fighting a bloody battle over control of the city of Monterrey, Mexico. The Americans were low on ammunition and someone had to carry that message to headquarters. Grant volunteered. He rode a horse through enemy fire along the

Crossing the Creek

streets of Monterrey. Thanks to his riding skills and luck, Grant delivered the message without suffering even a scratch.

Monterrey fell the next morning to the Americans, but the war continued. When Mexico refused to negotiate a surrender, President James K. Polk replaced Zachary Taylor with General Winfield Scott as commanding officer.

On March 9, 1847, Grant cheated death again. He and a group of army officers were scouting Mexican fortifications. One officer with him was a young Virginia man named Robert E. Lee. Just as Grant entered an adobe house, a shell hit the roof and exploded. Amazingly, Grant stumbled out of the wreckage without an injury.

While in the midst of the rigors of war, Grant received some happy news from St. Louis. Julia's father gave his permission for the couple to marry. In a letter dated August 4, Grant wrote to Julia, "You know how often I have asked you if your pa would give his consent to our engagement. I know now that he will and I am happy."[6]

Why did Colonel Dent finally give in and allow the soldier to marry his beloved daughter? Historians believe Dent was in debt and needed money. He was aware that the wealthy businessmen he had in mind as potential husbands for his daughter would not be interested in marrying into a financially unstable family. So he reluctantly relented.[7]

Ulysses S. Grant

Julia Dent and Ulysses S. Grant were married August 22, 1848.

Crossing the Creek

Meanwhile, the war was in its last stages. Two days after Scott's men entered the capital, Mexico City, on September 12, 1847, the fighting finally stopped. On September 16, Grant was named a first lieutenant. His bravery and praiseworthy conduct in battle were cited for the promotion. The war was officially over on February 2, 1848, when Mexico surrendered and signed a peace treaty with the United States.

Grant had much to celebrate that year. He returned home in July 1848 and a month later, on August 22, he and Julia were married at White Haven.

Grant later admitted he felt the Mexican War was wrong. Grant said he believed the war's main purpose was to keep as much territory where slavery would be legal in the United States as possible. He also felt that Mexico was not a threat to the well-being of the United States. Near the end of his life, Grant wrote in his memoirs, "I, to this day regard the war, which resulted, as one of the most unjust ever waged by a stronger against a weaker nation."[8]

He fought in the war, however, because it was his job. Grant wrote, "I considered my Supreme duty was to my flag."[9]

Grant spent the next few years stationed at army posts in Detroit, Michigan, and Sackets Harbor, New York. By fall 1849, Julia was pregnant with the couple's first child. At her doctor's suggestion, she returned to her family's home in St. Louis to have the baby. She gave birth to a son, Frederick Dent Grant, on May 30, 1850.

In the spring of 1852, Grant was ordered to an army base about three thousand miles from Sackets Harbor in Washington Territory. Since Julia was pregnant again, she stayed behind while Grant embarked on the long journey west. Before the invention of the telephone, news traveled very slowly. It was not until December 3 that Grant received word that Julia had given birth to their second child on July 22. It was a son named Ulysses S. Grant, Jr., who was called Buck.

Due to the cost and inconvenience of traveling so far, Julia stayed in St. Louis while her husband was on the West Coast. While away from his family, Grant began to drink heavily. According to historian Pam Sanfilippo, "He was very lonely, very depressed, he missed Julia, and there was not a lot going on. So like a lot of soldiers, he turned to drink."[10]

In a long overdue move in the fall of 1853, Grant was promoted to captain as an earned reward for his years of service in the army. He was told he would become commander of Company F, but it meant another move, this time to California. On January 5, 1854, Grant arrived at Fort Humboldt on the northern California coast. By now, his loneliness was too much to bear. On February 2, he wrote Julia and said, "You do not know how forsaken I feel here!"[11] About six weeks later, he said in another letter, "How very anxious I am to get home once again."[12] And once again, he relieved his loneliness by turning to alcohol.

Finally, on April 11, Grant resigned from the army.

Crossing the Creek

So he could tie up unfinished business matters, Grant stayed on duty until July 31. But he could not wait to be back with his family. He had given up on the idea of teaching mathematics and hoped to farm land Julia owned near White Haven. Grant told a friend, "Whoever hears of me in ten years, will hear of a well-to-do Missouri farmer."[13]

By now the Grants had one more mouth to feed. Julia gave birth to a daughter on July 4, 1855. She was named Ellen Wrenshall Grant, after Julia's mother, but was known as Nellie.

Upon his return to Missouri, Grant got busy on the farm. He worked alongside the Dents' slaves, and was

Ulysses S. Grant built this cabin and jokingly named it "Hardscrabble" because he was having trouble making it as a farmer.

often criticized for being too kind. Louisa Boggs, who was married to Julia's cousin, stated, "He was no hand to manage negroes. He couldn't force them to do anything. He wouldn't whip them."[14]

So the Grants could have some privacy, Julia's father helped them build their own log cabin on his property. Grant jokingly named it Hardscrabble. "Hardscrabble" is an adjective meaning barely surviving.

Unfortunately, there was more truth than humor in the name. Grant had trouble making money as a farmer. He tried to add to his meager farming income by taking a job hauling wood into the city. He seemed to enjoy those times when he would put on his old army overcoat, leave the farm for a day, and journey into St. Louis. In the city he could briefly forget the problems of farming and at times chat with old army buddies at the Jefferson Barracks. However, the time Grant spent hauling wood meant he spent less time tending to the needs of his farm, which hurt his income even more. By the time his fourth child, a son named Jesse Root Grant after Grant's father, was born on February 6, 1858, Grant was sinking deeper and deeper into debt. Later that year he fell ill with what was then called ague. It was a flulike illness with chills and a fever.

Giving up on farm life, Grant traded Hardscrabble for a house close to downtown St. Louis and took odd jobs, such as working for a real estate company and in a customs house. He had no better luck with those occupations than he did with farming.

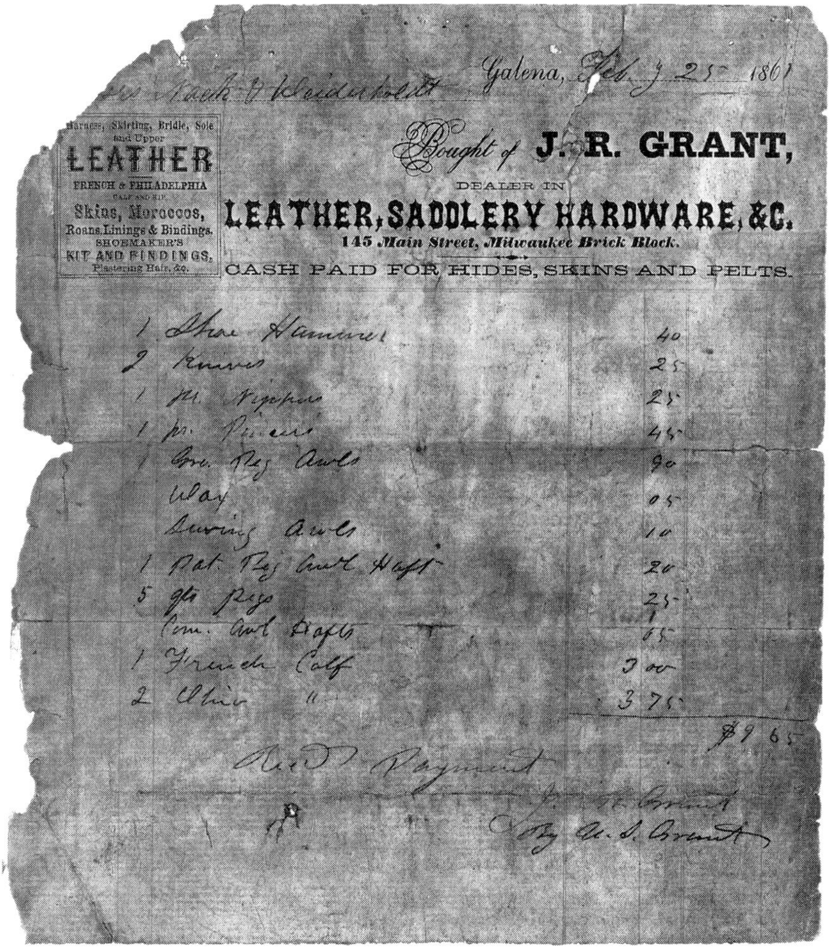

Galena, Feb. 25 1861

Harness, Skirting, Bridle, Sole and Upper
LEATHER
FRENCH & PHILADELPHIA
CALF AND KIP
Skins, Moroccos,
Roans, Linings & Bindings.
SHOEMAKER'S
KIT AND FINDINGS,
Plastering Hair, &c.

Bought of J. R. GRANT,
DEALER IN
LEATHER, SADDLERY HARDWARE, &C.
145 Main Street, Milwaukee Brick Block.
CASH PAID FOR HIDES, SKINS AND PELTS.

1	Shoe Hammer	40
2	Knives	25
1	pr. Nippers	25
1	pr. Pincers	45
1	Gro. Peg Awls	90
	Wax	05
	Sewing Awls	10
1	Pat. Peg Awl Haft	20
5	qts Pegs	25
	Com. Awl Hafts	05
1	French Calf	3 00
2	Ohio "	3 75
		$9 65

Rec'd Payment
J. R. Grant
By U. S. Grant

Grant gave up farming and chose to work as a clerk in his father's tannery store. A receipt dated 1861 shows what one could purchase at that time in a tannery.

Ulysses S. Grant

Grant's father, Jesse, was by then operating a tannery and store in Galena, Illinois, a town of hills and brick houses on the Mississippi River. Although Ulysses had never enjoyed tannery work, by now he had no choice. In order to make enough money to support his growing family, he took a job as a clerk in his father's store in Galena. Grant hoped he could finally settle down to raise his family in their own home.

So far he had been a failure at every occupation he had tried with one exception: the military. Perhaps Julia's father had been right all along when he suggested that this former army officer would never be able to support his daughter. But as had been the case fifteen years earlier, war was on the horizon, and Grant's life and his nation would soon be changed forever.

4

"HE *FIGHTS*"

Grant was toiling unhappily in his father's store in November 1860 when Abraham Lincoln was elected president of the United States. Lincoln opposed slavery and supported increased rights for African Americans. Slavery had been a way of life in the South for centuries, and many there believed they could not earn a living without slave labor.

While differences over slavery were one cause of the war, it was not the only one. The lives of the citizens of the North and the South had evolved in two completely different directions. The North was heavily industrialized and generally supported high tariffs, or taxes on imports, to protect the prices of goods they produced. While there were important cities in the South, such as Atlanta, Georgia; New Orleans, Louisiana; and

Charleston, South Carolina, the South's economy was based mainly on agriculture in the form of plantations. The livelihood of Southern residents relied on trade of their output, especially cotton, so the South generally favored low tariffs. In addition, they strongly supported the doctrine of states' rights, favoring more local rather than federal control over their lives.

The state of South Carolina took that concern to an extreme. It seceded, or formally withdrew, from the United States in December 1860. Over the next few months, ten more Southern states seceded and formed the Confederate States of America.

The Northern states felt it was vital that the nation stay united. Before long, the Civil War had begun.

When the North called for military volunteers, Grant enlisted. Thanks to Grant's background at West Point, in June 1861, Illinois governor Richard Yates appointed Grant a colonel. Grant was placed in charge of a regiment and led his men into Missouri in search of Confederate soldiers. He did not know it at the time, but Elihu Washburne, a congressman from his district in Illinois, suggested that Grant be made a brigadier general. Grant was appointed to that post, which he discovered while reading about it in a newspaper.

Most people in the North thought the South would quickly lose the war. On May 6, 1861, Grant wrote to his father, "My own opinion is that this war will be but of short duration, a few decisive victories in some of the

"He Fights"

Southern parts will send the secession army howling, and the leaders in the rebellion will flee the country."[1]

Brigadier General Grant led his force of about three thousand men to a victory on November 7, 1861, in Belmont, Missouri. In a battle lasting about four hours, his men subdued a Confederate regiment, forced them to retreat, and overtook their camp. Two months later, he convinced his commanding officer, General Henry W. Halleck, to allow him to attack the Confederates' Fort Henry in Tennessee. After an easy victory, Grant and his regiment took nearby Fort Donelson. These victories put

In 1861, the North, or Union, called for military volunteers. Grant enlisted and was appointed a colonel.

Ulysses S. Grant

two rivers, the Tennessee and the Cumberland, in Union hands.

Confederate general Simon Bolivar Buckner at Fort Donelson asked Grant for terms of surrender. Grant replied that he would accept nothing but an unconditional surrender. Grant suddenly had a new nickname: "Unconditional Surrender" Grant. It was a welcome change from "Useless Grant."

Grant led his men further south, but the Confederates were determined to stop them. By a log meetinghouse in Tennessee called Shiloh Church, the Confederates under General Albert Sidney Johnston took Grant by surprise and attacked his forces. The name *Shiloh* is a Hebrew word meaning "place of peace." But there was nothing peaceful about the events that began near the church on April 6, 1862.

The Union troops under Grant were nearly beaten. They suffered huge casualties, but reinforcements arrived in time, and Grant's men held off the Confederates. It was at a horrible cost, however. While the Confederates suffered over ten thousand casualties, the Union sustained over thirteen thousand.[2] Grant later recalled, "I saw an open field, so covered with dead that it would have been possible to walk across the clearing, in any direction, stepping on dead bodies, without a foot touching the ground."[3]

Grant now knew that it would not be a quick and easy war. General Halleck believed that there was no reason for so many casualties. He called for President

"*He* Fights"

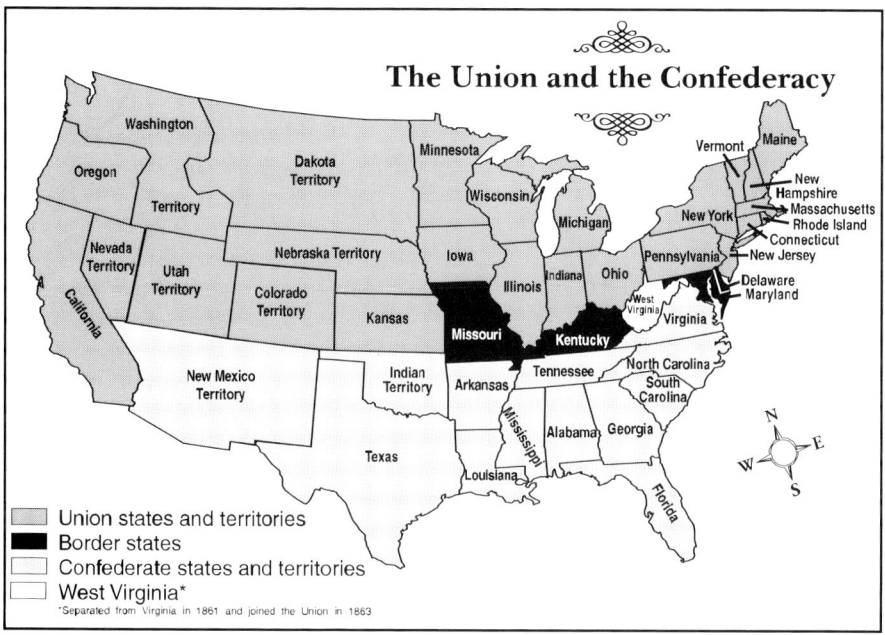

This map shows which states supported the Confederacy and which states supported the Union.

Lincoln to dismiss Grant. However, Lincoln replied very simply, "I can't spare this man; he *fights*."[4]

Some historians have said that Halleck tried to get rid of Grant because he was jealous of Grant's success. Halleck spread rumors about Grant recklessly drinking alcohol again. Grant became so disgusted with Halleck that he considered quitting the army. His good friend, General William Tecumseh Sherman, talked him out of it. Sherman chided him, "You could not be quiet at home for a week when armies are moving."[5]

Sherman also knew Grant was vital to the Union's cause. Other Union generals, such as General George McClellan, were hesitant to take action when needed.

That led to early Union defeats. However, historian Shelby Foote noted, "Grant the general has many qualities, but he has a thing that's very necessary for a great general. He had what they call 'four o'clock in the morning courage.' You could wake him up at four o'clock in the morning and tell him they had just turned his right flank and he would be as cool as a cucumber."[6]

Yet his poor judgment seemed to constantly get him into trouble. In late 1862, Jesse Grant came to visit his son, then camped in western Tennessee. Jesse brought with him some friends, an Ohio family whose last name was Mack. At first Grant welcomed the Macks. He then learned that they were in the cotton business and were using Grant to have access to cotton supplies in areas under his supervision.

Grant immediately sent the Macks away. Once he learned they were Jewish, Grant wrote an order that, according to historian Jean Edward Smith was, "one of the most blatant examples of state-sponsored anti-Semitism [anti-Jewish prejudice] in American history."[7] The beginning of the order read, "The Jews, as a class violating every regulation of trade established by the Treasury Department and also department orders, are hereby expelled from the department within twenty-four hours from receipt of this order."[8]

The order was put into effect, and Jews in the area were made to leave. In Paducah, Kentucky, thirty Jewish families were forced out of their homes. Some supported Grant, since the mid-nineteenth century was a time

SOURCE DOCUMENT

HERE'S TO THE TANNER'S SON.

COMPOSED BY

GEORGE WM. STEWART, of New-York City.

Dedicated to the Soldiers of the Union.

Here's to the Tanner's son,
For that was his vocation;
He is hearty and strong
To tan the cause of treason and rebellion.
He has fought them on the river,
He has fought them on the plain,
He whips them when he meets them,
And he will whip them again!

The powers that be, President Abraham Lincoln,
Sent for him to come to Washington;
They dined him, they piped him,
To know his business in Washington.
His answer was to questioners all,
On business for the nation,
To the President, the work could be done
With plans of his own, with troops, and let alone.

He is plain and honest, hearty and strong,
His soldiers they adore him,
The people they are all for him;
We will place him in the chair of Washington,
The saviour of our common country.
In the chair he will set things straight,
Which by military necessity
Have long been set at naught.

No traitor knaves nor cheating politicians
For offices under him need apply,
He will know whom to trust,
Those who in the battle front have bled the military;
Now the war is over, our work as soldiers is done,
As citizens to set straight the laws and Constitution.
Four years more with anxious care,
Will bring back the States where they were.

Due to Grant's popularity as a Union general, songs were written about him.

when anti-immigrant and pro-white Protestant feelings ran strong. However, the overwhelming reaction was outrage by both Jews and Gentiles. Newspaper editorials blasted Grant's order as something that had no place in the United States, especially considering that the nation was fighting for people's freedom. As soon as President Lincoln was made aware of the order, he demanded that Grant revoke it without hesitation. Grant did so on January 6, 1863. Whether Grant harbored true anti-Jewish feelings or whether he issued the order in an unwise moment of anger continues to be debated by historians.

While Grant's Vicksburg campaign was reaching a climax in early July 1863, the turning point of the war was taking place hundreds of miles east in Gettysburg, Pennsylvania. Confederate general Robert E. Lee had been trying to invade the North. Lee commanded the Confederate Army of Northern Virginia and had led it to numerous victories against the Union. He was regarded by many as the smartest military mind among the Confederates.

On July 1, 1863, Lee's army met up with General George Meade's Union Army of the Potomac in Gettysburg. The armies battled for three days in bloody, hand-to-hand combat. The results were a body-strewn battlefield and a retreat by Lee and his forces. Meade did not pursue Lee, allowing him to fight on and for the war to continue.

Now that the Union controlled the Mississippi River,

"*He* Fights"

they set their sights on other strategic locations in the Confederacy. Chattanooga, in the southeastern corner of Tennessee near the Georgia border, sat at the junction of two important railroads. For that reason, the Union felt it was necessary to gain control of Chattanooga. Union general William S. Rosecrans was in charge of Union troops there. On September 19, 1863, Rosecrans led his army from Chattanooga a few miles away to Chickamauga Creek, where they met an army of Confederates led by General Braxton Bragg. Bragg's Southern army hit Rosecrans's army hard, causing Rosecrans and his men to retreat back to Chattanooga.

Grant was called to replace Rosecrans and on November 24, 1863, he commenced what became known as the Battle of Chattanooga. Two days later, Grant's army had defeated Bragg's army, and the Confederates retreated into Georgia. Chattanooga was in Union hands, and a short while later became the supply base for General William Tecumseh Sherman's army.

In March 1864, Grant journeyed to Washington, D.C. The morning of March 8 dawned gray and dreary, but for Grant it was the sunniest of days. President Lincoln awarded Grant the rank of lieutenant general and placed him in command of all the armies in the field. It was a truly special honor and an awesome responsibility. But the short, bearded soldier had no time to savor his new post. From Washington, he headed south into Virginia, where he was needed for an even more dangerous campaign against the skilled Robert E. Lee.

Union men who had fought in previous Virginia campaigns felt Grant would be facing his toughest competitor in General Lee. Lee proved to be a strong rival, but Grant was no less tough. Whether or not it was because of his superstition about retracing his steps, Grant would not retreat. He and Lee fought bloody battles in Virginia in the spring of 1864, as Grant slowly forced Lee's armies south. In just six weeks, the Union lost sixty thousand men.[9]

People in the North were outraged over the huge loss of life and blamed Grant. One of his critics was the president's wife, Mary Todd Lincoln. The first lady said, "Grant is a butcher and not fit to be at the head of an army. He loses two men to the enemy's one. He has no management, no regard for life, I could fight an army as well myself."[10]

But Grant persevered. He trapped Lee outside Petersburg, Virginia, south of Richmond. A siege began and lasted ten months. Finally, on April 1, 1865, Petersburg fell to the Union. The Confederates abandoned their capital, Richmond. Lee fled west along the Appomattox River, and Grant pursued him the entire way. Finally, Lee surrendered to Grant at the town of Appomattox Court House on April 9.

The two generals met in the brick home of a man named Wilmer McLean. Lee looked dignified in his gray uniform. Grant had a sloppy appearance, wearing a

SOURCE DOCUMENT

We, the undersigned Prisoners of War, belonging to the Army of Northern Virginia, having been this day surrendered by General Robert E. Lee, C. S. A., Commanding said Army, to Lieut. Genl. U. S. Grant, Commanding Armies of United States, do hereby give our solemn parole of honor that we will not hereafter serve in the armies of the Confederate States, or in any military capacity whatever, against the United States of America, or render aid to the enemies of the latter, until properly exchanged, in such manner as shall be mutually approved by the respective authorities.

Done at Appomattox Court House, Va., this 9th day of April, 1865.

After months of battle between the North and the South, Confederate general Robert E. Lee surrendered to General Ulysses S. Grant on April 9, 1965, in Appomattox Court House, Virginia.

Ulysses S. Grant

SOURCE DOCUMENT

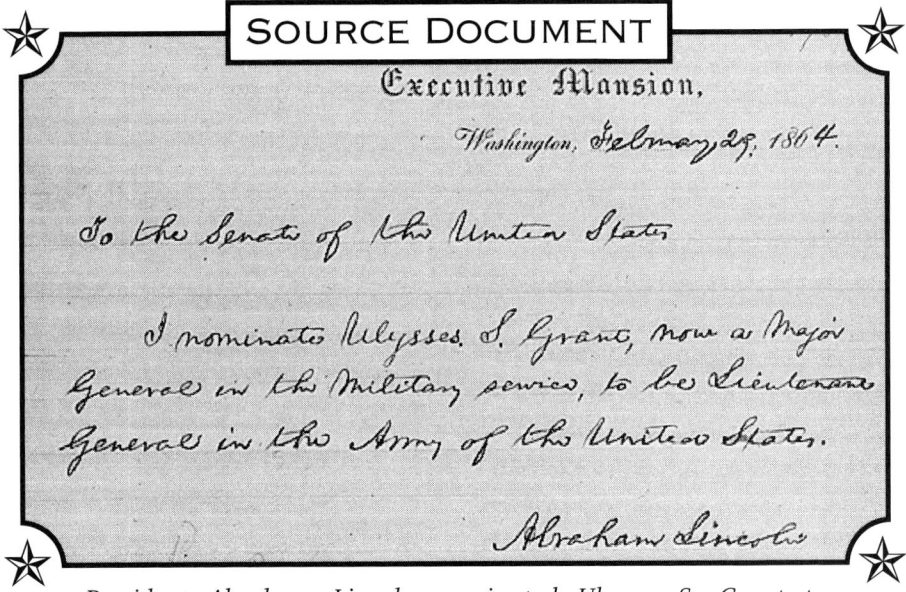

President Abraham Lincoln nominated Ulysses S. Grant to Lieutenant General of the Army.

private's jacket and with his boots and pants splattered with mud. The two men shook hands. Grant reminded Lee that they had served together in the Mexican War nearly twenty years earlier.

Grant offered Lee generous terms. He allowed the Confederate officers to keep their side arms and personal possessions. Since it was planting season, Grant permitted all Confederate soldiers to keep their horses and mules. Grant also ordered food rations to feed the starving Southerners. Grant and Lee shook hands again. Lee left the house first, then Grant.

As Grant walked away from the McLean House, Union troops cheered and fired guns in celebration. Grant put a stop to that. He announced, "The war is over. The Rebels are our countrymen again."[11]

5

"Let Us Have Peace"

Just five days after Grant left Appomattox, President and Mrs. Lincoln invited the general and his wife to join them in attending the play *Our American Cousin* in Washington. The general told the president with regret that he could not join him. He wanted to return home to Burlington, New Jersey, to see his children.

It is believed by some that Grant's real reason for turning down the president was that Julia did not get along with Mary Lincoln and did not want to spend an evening with her.[1] A recently-engaged couple were invited instead.

That night, a little after 10 P.M., an actor named John Wilkes Booth snuck into the president's theater box and shot him in the head. Who knows what would have

Ulysses S. Grant

When President Lincoln was assassinated in 1865, Vice President Andrew Johnson (right) became president. In 1862, Lincoln had appointed Johnson military governor of Tennessee. The following election year, Johnson was Lincoln's running mate.

happened to the Grants if they had been seated next to the Lincolns that night.

Lincoln died the next morning, and Vice President Andrew Johnson became president. Johnson was a senator from Tennessee when his state seceded from the Union in 1861. In fact, Johnson was the only senator from a Confederate state not to support secession.[2] In 1862, Lincoln appointed him military governor of Tennessee.

Two years later, Lincoln selected Johnson as his running mate for reelection. Even though Johnson was a Democrat, he honored Lincoln's wishes. When Lincoln

"Let Us Have Peace"

was reelected that November, Johnson became his vice president.

When Johnson became president, it was a time of chaos and confusion in America. The South was in ruins. Many buildings stood empty, with broken windows and vandalized interiors. With the Confederacy defeated, its money was worthless. Weeds had taken over the cotton fields on plantation grounds. Slaves were now free, and Southern landowners had to look hard to find workers. And what would the former slaves do? Where would they go? Many could not read or write. How could they support themselves?

This was the situation Johnson faced. Meanwhile, the Civil War was technically not finished. When Robert E. Lee surrendered, the South lost its biggest army. But in North Carolina, a Confederate army under General Joseph E. Johnston continued fighting. Johnston surrendered April 26, 1865, to General Sherman. The war was then finally and officially over.

Several senators from the North wanted to severely punish the South for seceding from the Union. They considered

After the Civil War, Ulysses S. Grant was considered a military hero.

Ulysses S. Grant

its actions to be treasonous. These senators were called Radical Republicans. Although Lincoln was a Republican, he did not believe strong punishment was the answer. He felt that by being lenient, things in the United States would return to normal as quickly as possible.

Andrew Johnson believed the same. He said, "If a state is to be nursed until it again gets strength, it must be nursed by its friends, not smothered by its enemies."[3] In May 1865, Johnson granted amnesty to all Confederates except for those who had been war leaders. That meant they could not be punished for treason or a similar crime. All they had to do was take an oath of allegiance to the United States.

Like most Southerners, Johnson believed strongly in states' rights. Johnson sacrificed that belief during the war in order to keep the nation together. Jim Small, a historian and chief of interpretation at Andrew Johnson National Historic Site in Greeneville, Tennessee, said, "Once the war was over, Johnson felt strongly that all the powers needed to return to the states."[4]

The Radical Republicans felt the opposite—that the federal government should have the bulk of the power. They feared that laws made by the Southern states would be unfair to freed slaves.

The period known as Reconstruction had begun. Federal troops were sent to the South with the purpose of helping rebuild the devastated area and assisting

"Let Us Have Peace"

African Americans in adjusting to a new way of life after slavery.

The Northern troops were not welcome by many in the South. In December 1865, a secret society called the Ku Klux Klan was formed in Pulaski, Tennessee. Its purpose was to terrorize and murder African Americans so they would be too scared to claim their rights as United States citizens.

During this time, Grant was touring the country and accepting honors for his part in the Union victory. People in cities across the United States rewarded him with everything from money to horses. The people of Philadelphia, Pennsylvania, and Galena, Illinois, went so far as to present Grant with brand new homes. It was probably the most happy time in his life.[5] However, whether Grant liked it or not, he would soon become involved in politics. People were already considering him as a candidate for president of the United States.

Congress under Johnson was dominated by Republicans who sent the president a series of bills which strongly penalized the South. Other bills favored the federal government over states' rights. Some were supported only by Radical Republicans, while others were backed by moderates, too. But Johnson vetoed, or rejected, one bill after another. In doing so, Johnson became viewed by even moderate Republicans as stubborn and unwilling to compromise. "Congress and Andrew Johnson simply didn't understand each other," said historian Jim Small.[6]

Ulysses S. Grant

As Grant toured the United States, people rewarded him with honors, money, and even houses, like this one in Galena, Illinois. This was a very happy time in his life. But like it or not, Grant was soon to enter into politics.

"Let Us Have Peace"

At first Grant supported Johnson, but was now losing faith in him. Grant soon sided with the Congressional Republicans over the president.

In the summer of 1866, Johnson decided it would be a good strategy to travel through the North to firm up political support. In order to impress the people, Johnson took Grant and other Civil War heroes with him.

Little did Johnson know that the trip would be a total disaster. Jim Small notes, "It turned into an embarrassment for Johnson because everyone wanted to hear Grant speak. Grant won the war, not Johnson. The trip backfired."[7]

In July of that year, Grant was given a special promotion no American had been given in eighty years, the rank of full general. Grant was the first person since George Washington to hold that title.

That November, Americans voted for many new members of Congress, and Republicans won enough seats to be able to override Johnson's vetoes. After the president vetoes a bill, Congress votes on it once more. If two thirds of Congress approves it, the bill is passed over the president's veto.

Congress took advantage of its sudden power. A bill introduced by Radical Republican senator Thaddeus Stevens of Pennsylvania called for military government in all Southern states except for Tennessee, which had been admitted back into the Union under Lincoln.

One reason for Stevens's bill was the continuing

violence and lawlessness in the South at the hands of the Ku Klux Klan. Johnson vetoed the bill as being too harsh, but Congress overrode it. The bill became law on March 2, 1867.

That same day, Congress passed a bill greatly limiting presidential power. It said that the president could not issue any orders to the army unless they went through the general in command. At the time, the general in command happened to be Grant. Congress then passed another bill, the Tenure of Office Act. That would come close to ruining Johnson's presidency.

The Tenure of Office Act stated that any person holding an office that took Senate approval could not be replaced unless his replacement was also approved by the Senate. Its purpose was to keep Johnson from replacing Radical Republicans with states' rights Democrats.

Johnson ignored the new law. Edwin M. Stanton had been secretary of war since 1862 and was one of the most extreme Radical Republicans. Johnson felt he could not have someone with whom he disagreed so strongly in his Cabinet. In the summer of 1867, the president asked Stanton to resign. Stanton refused, so Johnson fired him and replaced him with Grant.

When Congress met in December, they passed a resolution saying that according to the Tenure of Office Act, Johnson's firing of Stanton was illegal. Stanton, they claimed, was still secretary of war. As soon as Grant

"Let Us Have Peace"

got word of the resolution, he stepped down, allowing Stanton his old job back.

Johnson could not have been angrier at Grant. He felt Grant should have held onto the job, or at least stayed on until Johnson could name his own replacement.

Grant replied in a letter that he believed that by stepping down he was obeying the law. He added that he had planned to give Johnson time to find a replacement, but was so busy with the many duties of his office that he never got around to it. To Johnson's supporters, that sounded like the weakest of excuses.

Johnson would not back down. He fired Stanton again. To the Republicans in Congress, this was too much. They voted to impeach Johnson.

Impeachment is a concept dating to the earliest days of the United States. The United States Constitution reads, "The President, Vice President and all civil Officers of the United States, shall be removed from Office on Impeachment for, and Conviction of, Treason, Bribery, or other high Crimes and Misdemeanors."

The House of Representatives would vote whether to officially charge the president with an impeachable offense. If such charges were approved by the House, then a trial would take place before the United States Senate with the Senate acting as a jury. If two thirds of the Senate voted to convict the president on any charge, the president would be removed from office.

Johnson was not accused of treason or bribery, but

Ulysses S. Grant

his opponents said that his disregard of the Tenure of Office Act fell in the category of "high crimes and misdemeanors." In his defense, Johnson maintained that the Tenure of Office Act was unconstitutional. He claimed that as chief executive he was legally responsible for the secretary of war's actions and therefore held the power of appointments and firings.

The case was tried before the Senate in the spring of 1868. On May 16, the Senate voted on Johnson's fate. The total vote was thirty-five guilty and nineteen not guilty, barely short of the two thirds needed for removal from office.[8] Johnson was saved by one vote.

It was a hollow victory since Johnson had less than a year left of his presidency. The Republican National Convention was held on May 20, just four days after the impeachment vote. Grant was the obvious choice as the nominee for president. He chose as his running mate Speaker of the House Schuyler Colfax of Indiana. Their campaign slogan was "Let Us Have Peace."

The damaged Johnson was not renominated by the Democrats. Instead they selected former New York governor Horatio Seymour. Seymour campaigned in favor of states' rights and charged the Republicans in Congress of being too radical. Seymour and the Democrats also criticized Grant personally as an alcoholic and someone not smart enough to hold the highest office in the nation.

In response, Grant and the Republicans condemned the Democrats as the party of the Confederacy.

"Let Us Have Peace"

A pro-Republican newspaper, the *New York Tribune*, wrote, "Scratch a Democrat, and you'll find a rebel under his skin."⁹ They also claimed that Seymour was in poor health and had insanity in his family.

When the votes were counted, Grant had 3,012,833 to Seymour's 2,703,249. Grant won 214 electoral votes. Seymour won 80.¹⁰ The 1868 election was the first in which African Americans could legally vote, and their ballots helped Grant and Colfax win several Southern states. Grant was sworn in as president of the United States on March 4, 1869. He never could have realized what lay before him.

6

NO KING MIDAS

The American people were thrilled to have Grant as their leader. At only forty-six, Ulysses S. Grant was the youngest president elected up to that time.[1] Unlike those who had been involved in the impeachment crisis, Grant was not a professional politician. Many Americans thought it would be good for the country to have a president who had never been involved in the backbiting business of politics.

Yet, almost as soon as Grant took the oath of office on March 4, 1869, some citizens began to have doubts. Grant did not choose the most qualified people for his Cabinet. He selected friends and others who had supported his campaign with donations. It did not seem to matter to Grant whether they were smart or hard working, only that they had backed him during his presidential run.

SOURCE DOCUMENT

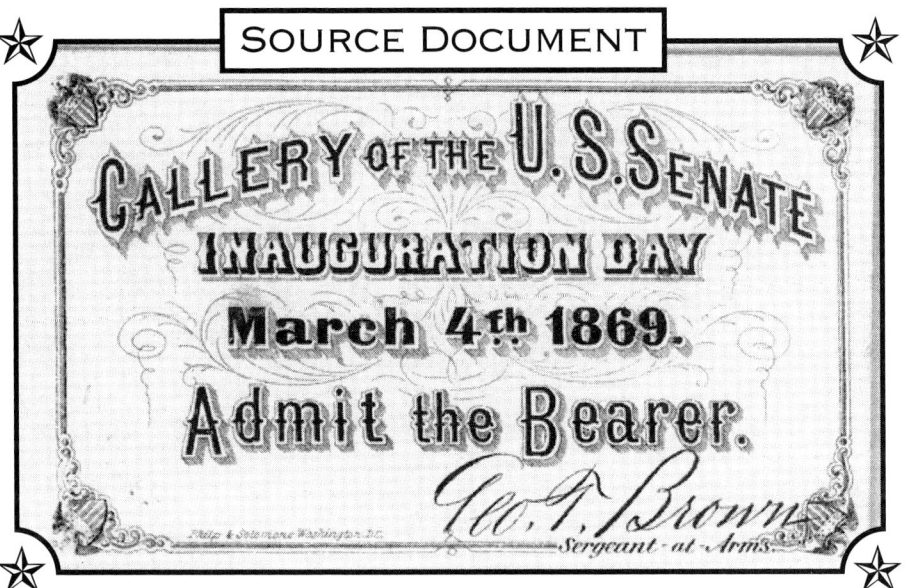

Ulysses S. Grant was elected the eighteenth president of the United States and took the oath of office on March 4, 1869. This ticket admitted people to the inauguration day ceremonies.

One example was his choice for secretary of state. The secretary of state deals with representatives from foreign countries and must be a very skilled diplomat. Grant chose Elihu Washburne, the Illinois congressman who had suggested him for the office of brigadier general in 1861. Washburne was neither well educated nor a skilled diplomat, and he stayed at the job for only a week. Several other Cabinet members did poorly at their jobs and also resigned.

Just a month after he took office, Grant brought up the idea of annexing the Caribbean island nation of Santo Domingo, today the Dominican Republic. A Civil War friend, Admiral David Ammen, thought it would be a perfect place for an American naval base. The leaders of Santo Domingo believed they could use the United States's financial help. In addition, Grant thought former slaves could be relocated there, away from the Ku Klux Klan and other extremists in the United States.

Grant's new secretary of state was a respected man named Hamilton Fish, who should have been the person to negotiate with Santo Domingo. But Fish became sick before he was about to leave, so Grant sent his personal military secretary, Colonel Orville E. Babcock, in Fish's place. Babcock was as enthusiastic about annexing Santo Domingo as Grant. In July, Babcock boarded a boat and headed south to negotiate the deal with Santo Domingo.

Meanwhile, in Washington, some shrewd businessmen realized that while Grant may have made a superb general, he did not possess sharp political skills. One of the wealthiest men in the country was Jay Gould, who had made a fortune in railroads, shipping, and investing. Gould and a financier named James Fisk went out of their way to become friendly with Grant's brother-in-law, Abel R. Corbin. They did not care about Corbin's friendship but used him to get to the president. Gould and Fisk's aim was to try to corner the gold market to get even richer than they already were.

Abel Corbin was no fool. He knew what Gould and Fisk wanted, and Corbin wanted something in return. So Gould and Fisk paid him twenty-five thousand dollars and promised him a share of any future money they made from their scheme.

SOURCE DOCUMENT

(1)

Citizens of the United States:

Your suffrage having elevated me to the office of President of the United States I have, in conformity with to the Constitution of our country, taken the oath of office prescribed therein. I have taken this oath without mental reservation, with the determination to do, to the best of my ability, all that it requires of me. The responsibilities of the position I feel, but accept them without fear. The office has to me unsought. I commence its duties untrammelled. I wish

After Ulysses S. Grant was sworn in as president, he gave this speech to the citizens of the United States.

Corbin then convinced the president that higher gold prices would be good for American farmers. Corbin argued that the new prices would allow farmers to get the best value when selling their products overseas.

Gould and Fisk then met with the president on a steamboat on Long Island Sound, outside New York City. This was not a private ship, but part of a public line Gould owned. The three men sipped on brandy and champagne, and smoked fine cigars as Gould and Fisk emphasized Corbin's points about the high price of gold as beneficial to farmers. Gould and Fisk purposely chose to meet in a public place so it would seem to observers that Grant was working with them.

In the past, when the price of gold climbed too high, the United States Treasury sold some to keep the price stable. After meeting with the two financiers, Grant told the Treasury not to sell off gold as it normally did. On Friday, September 24, 1869, Fisk and Gould bought huge amounts of gold, causing the price of the precious metal to soar. As a result, there was a huge financial panic on the New York Stock Exchange. Many businesses went bankrupt as a result. The day became known as Black Friday.

When Grant realized he had been a dupe in Gould and Fisk's plan, he ordered the United States Treasury to free up $4 million worth of gold to be sold to the public. The gold market then stabilized, but the damage had been done. Only six months into his term of office, the president of the United States was viewed by many

SOURCE DOCUMENT

Union Pacific Railroad Company
Sears Building

Boston Sept 30 1869

Sir:

I have the honor to transmit herewith the Annual Report of the Union Pacific Railroad Company for year ending June 30/69.

A change having taken place in the office of the General Superintendent subsequent to that date, we are as yet without the Report from that Department, but will forward it as soon as written, by the present incumbent.

Having just returned from a trip over the Road with the Late Commission, it has been impossible to furnish this Report at an earlier day.—

I have the honor to be
Most Respectfully
Your obdt servt
Oliver Ames
Presdt Union Pacific R.R. Co.

Hon J. D. Cox,
Secretary of Interior
Washington, D.C.

Grant chose many friends for his Cabinet. One he chose was former governor of Ohio Jacob D. Cox for secretary of interior. This letter from the Union Pacific Railroad is addressed to Cox.

as an ignorant and naive man who allowed unethical people to take advantage of him.

On December 21, 1869, Colonel Babcock presented a formal treaty to annex Santo Domingo to Grant and his Cabinet. On January 10, 1870, the president sent the treaty to the Senate. In order for it to pass, Grant felt he needed help from the chairman of the Senate Foreign Relations Committee, Massachusetts senator Charles Sumner.

Grant met privately with Sumner to persuade him to support the treaty. Sumner was a fiercely proud man, and he and Grant had never gotten along well. In their meeting, Grant made things worse. In an absentminded manner, four times Grant referred to Sumner as the chairman of the wrong committee, the Judiciary Committee. Sumner found Grant's repeated error to be very annoying.[2] Yet Sumner listened to the president's argument in favor of annexing Santo Domingo. When Grant was about to leave, the senator told him, "Mr. President, I am an Administration man, and whatever you do will always find in me the most careful and candid consideration."[3]

The president assumed that statement meant he had Sumner's vote.[4] However, Sumner said he meant only that he would carefully consider the treaty. When the treaty came to a vote, Sumner came out against it. One reason was that he believed that African Americans should be treated as equals in their own country and not be shipped to some Caribbean island. Grant felt Sumner had double-crossed him. From then on, he never passed Sumner's house without shaking his fist.[5] The treaty was debated in the Senate over the next few months. Without Sumner's support, the treaty to annex Santo Domingo was defeated on June 30, 1870.

The president also had his hands full at home. On February 3, 1870, Congress ratified the Fifteenth Amendment to the Constitution, which stated that citizens of the United States should not be denied the right to vote because of their race. A problem was how to enforce the new law. In the South, the Ku Klux Klan and other extremists were using violence to keep African Americans from living peacefully and exercising their civil rights as citizens. They were also terrorizing white Republicans. On May 31, Grant received support from Congress when the lawmakers passed the first in a series of laws known as the Enforcement Acts. It "banned the use of force, bribery, or intimidation to interfere with the right to vote and prohibited state officials from discriminating among voters on the basis of race."[6]

Those accused of breaking this law would be tried in federal courts, where a fair trial was more likely to take place. In a state trial in the South, it would have been easy to pack a jury with people who did not want African Americans to have equal rights.

Even though Congress had passed the Enforcement Act, the government either did not have the money or manpower to carry out the law. Reports of threats, beatings, and even murders of innocent African Americans and their supporters continued. They became so frequent that in December 1870 Congress began an investigation.

On April 20, 1871, Congress passed what became known as the Ku Klux Klan Act. Its purpose was to enforce the Fourteenth Amendment of the United States Constitution. That amendment, adopted during Andrew Johnson's term in 1868, says among other declarations, that Americans' rights of citizenship cannot be restricted and no state can make and enforce any law taking away their privileges or depriving them of "life, liberty, or property, without due process of law." One major purpose in approving the amendment was to ensure newly freed slaves had full rights and that no state could enact its own laws to take those rights away.

The Ku Klux Klan Act allowed the government to revoke a legal order called *habeas corpus* in places where the local police could not or would not protect citizens' rights. *Habeas corpus* permits the release of a person being held against his or her liberty without "probable cause," or proof of guilt. Basically, it means a person is entitled to a hearing to determine whether he or she should continue to be held. *Habeas corpus*, or the right to such a hearing, was denied in this case for the purpose of maintaining order. The same act also permitted the president to impose martial law, or law enforced by military police or agents. Martial law is usually in place in only the most extreme situations.

No King Midas

While not making the best decisions in his Cabinet appointments, Grant made some strides in civil rights of now-free African Americans. In 1871, Congress passed the Ku Klux Klan Act, which allowed the government to revoke habeas corpus *and impose martial law in areas where extremists were threatening African Americans.*

The United States had other Civil War-related matters to attend to. During the war, Great Britain had sided with the Confederacy, and the Confederate states purchased some warships from the British. Five in particular, the *Alabama, Florida, Georgia, Rappahannock,* and *Shenandoah,* caused much damage to the Union. Now the United States wanted reparations, or money to cover the harm the British ships had done.

It was the job of Secretary of State Hamilton Fish to negotiate with British ambassador to the United States

Sir Edward Thornton over the amount of money Britain would pay. Senator Charles Sumner wanted to charge the British over $2 billion.[7] Fish knew there was no way Thornton would say yes to such a huge amount. After much discussion, Fish and Thornton agreed on a total of $15.5 million.[8] The agreement became known as the Treaty of Washington, and it was signed May 8, 1871. The Senate overwhelmingly approved it by a vote of fifty to twelve on May 24, and it was ratified in London, England, on June 17.[9]

That victory was offset by the continued crimes against African Americans in the South. Some of the worst attacks took place in South Carolina. Grant made an example of the state by suspending *habeas corpus* and sending federal troops to the state. Several arrests were made and order was resumed for a while. Yet it was nearly impossible to keep enforcing the law throughout the entire South since African Americans were continually threatened and attacked and there were never enough troops available to prevent it or catch suspected assailants.

Every president has had his own personal manner of fulfilling his duties. As for Grant, no one ever accused him of working too hard. He often started his workday about 10:00 A.M. and stopped about 3:00 P.M. He spent late afternoons in the presidential stables where he would pass the time with his favorite animals. A White House clerk named William Crook wrote, "I think no man ever separated his business life from his social life more completely than Grant. He seemed an entirely different man when friends were around him. That does not mean that he was talkative or that he laughed very often, but he was genial and full of content."[10]

Crook also recalled that Grant was a loving father and devoted to his wife, Julia. "I have never seen a more devoted family or a happier one. I am sure he thought she [Julia] was absolutely perfect. He couldn't get along without his wife."[11]

Whether the nation could get along without him was another matter. The next year was an election year, and there were more troubles on the way for the president.

7

A Victory, a Panic, and a Wedding

★ ★ ★

Grant began to concentrate on running for reelection as 1871 turned into 1872. The year 1872 marked Grant's fourth year in office, and as is the law in the United States, a presidential election was scheduled for November.

Sitting presidents have often been renominated by their parties. Ulysses S. Grant would not have it so easy. Several of the nation's best-known Republicans thought Grant was a disaster as a president. These included Chief Justice of the Supreme Court Salmon P. Chase, former ambassador to England Charles Francis Adams, and editor of the *New York Tribune* Horace Greeley. (It was Greeley who became famous for coining the famous phrase, "Go west, young man," his way of urging settlers to make new homes in the vast American West.)

A Victory, a Panic, and a Wedding

These Republicans referred to themselves as Liberal Republicans and were more moderate than the Radical Republicans. They felt military reconstruction of the South should end right away. They were also disheartened by the failures and controversies during Grant's first administration. They had no doubt that Grant was an honest person, but they believed he was a poor judge of character and was in over his head as president. The Liberal Republicans demanded drastic reform of the civil service system, the method of awarding government jobs.

The Liberal Republicans did something unusual in 1872. They broke from their party and held a separate convention in Cincinnati, Ohio, where they chose to nominate their own candidate for president.

But who would they choose? They debated several possible candidates' names at their convention. Yet when the voting took place, none received enough votes to be nominated. So they voted again, and four more times. Finally, on the sixth ballot, the delegates settled on a compromise candidate, newspaper editor Horace Greeley.

Although the Liberal Republicans now had a candidate, he was not without problems. Greeley seemed to many as weak as Grant, but without Grant's four years of presidential experience. He was also seen as an eccentric man completely unqualified for the presidency. Historian Paul Boller has described Greeley as "erratic,

Ulysses S. Grant

While the 1872 election was drawing near, Grant did not have an easy time being renominated. Many of his fellow Republicans did not think he was doing a good job because of scandals and controversies. They split from the party to become Liberal Republicans. The Liberal Republicans nominated their own candidate at a separate convention.

A Victory, a Panic, and a Wedding

crotchety, unpredictable, and thoroughly incompetent in the art of politics."[1]

The rest of the Republican party had its convention one month later in Philadelphia. Grant was renominated with ease, but he dropped Schuyler Colfax as his running mate. Colfax was one of many Grant friends linked to scandals. In Colfax's place, Grant chose Senator Henry Wilson from Natick, Massachusetts. Like the Liberal Republicans, their platform called for civil service reform. It also called for equal rights for all American citizens regardless of color.

Finally, that summer the Democrats met for their convention in Baltimore. It was a bizarre political gathering. The Democrats met for only six hours and decided not to nominate their own candidate. Instead, they supported the Liberal Republicans' nominee, Horace Greeley. They wanted anyone who could beat Grant, and Greeley seemed like the best bet.

The campaign was nasty. Grant supporters portrayed Greeley as a doddering old man and a traitor to his party. Those favoring Greeley called Grant a corrupt alcoholic. A history professor named Eugene H. Roseboom said of the 1872 election, "Never in American history have two more unfit men been offered to the country for the highest office."[2]

To most voters, Grant, with his presidential experience, seemed the lesser of two evils. Then, about six weeks before the election, word got out about more corruption under Grant's watch. Just as computers are

Ulysses S. Grant

the biggest industry today, railroads were the newest thing when Grant was president. The first transcontinental railroad had just been completed in 1869.

In any cutting-edge business, there is much money to be made. However, there are always risks involved. For every person who has gotten incredibly wealthy in companies related to the computer industry, many more have lost money. The same was true regarding the railroad industry in President Grant's day. And as in all times, there were people who wanted to make money dishonestly.

A construction company involved in building the Union Pacific Railroad had the unusual name of Credit Mobilier. The Union Pacific was to be one of the major rail lines in the country, and it was funded by the United States government through people's taxes. For some time, officers of Credit Mobilier were stealing company profits. To keep Congress from investigating their illegal activities, the Credit Mobilier officers bribed several members of Congress. A bribe is a payment of money or gifts given to a person in power with the expectation of special favors in return.

The bribe Credit Mobilier officers offered to several important members of Congress came in the form of company stocks. Stocks are portions, or shares, of a business. If a company makes money, the person who buys stock in that company receives some of that profit.

Most historians believe that Grant had nothing to do with the scandal. However, Greeley supporters tried

A Victory, a Panic, and a Wedding

their best to tie Grant to it. They said that even if Grant was honest, he was so unaware of the dishonest practices going on under his watch that he was unfit to lead. With Greeley as president, they campaigned, nobody would be able to get away with crimes like these.

Most voters seemed to think that Greeley was taking advantage of the scandal just to help his election campaign.[3] Then, just days before the American people went to vote, Greeley's wife died.

The voters overwhelmingly elected Grant to a second term as president. He received over 55 percent of the vote, to Greeley's 44 percent, and 286 electoral votes to Greeley's 66.[4] The strange election of 1872 took another bizarre turn three weeks later when Greeley himself died on November 29. Grant graciously attended Greeley's funeral.

Grant saw his reelection as proof that the American people forgave him for any mistakes he had made as president.[5] Yet as soon as Grant's second term began, the same kind of problems emerged.

On its last day in session, Congress voted a pay raise for itself and the president. Senators and representatives increased their yearly income from five thousand dollars to seven thousand five hundred dollars. The president's salary was raised from twenty-five thousand dollars to fifty thousand dollars a year.[6]

What shocked the citizens was that Congress also voted to give the raise to congressmen who were defeated in the 1872 election. They would get extra pay for the two years they had served before the new law was ratified.

Congress attached the pay raise to a bigger and more important bill. Grant could not veto the pay raise without vetoing the entire bill. Since it was the last day of the session, there would be no time to rework the bill should Grant veto it. Grant had little choice but to sign it. The citizens were outraged by what became known as the "salary grab," or "back-pay grab." In response to the American people's anger, some members of Congress returned their extra back pay to the government. Still, the fact that the law had been passed seemed to be one more example of corruption under Grant.

That was not all the people were angry about. That same year, Secretary of the Treasury William A. Richardson selected a friend named John D. Sanborn to collect delinquent, or late, taxes. For doing his job, Sanborn was legally allowed to keep half of what he collected. At first, Sanborn did his job honestly.

In time, Richardson gave Sanborn permission to collect much more than just delinquent taxes. Sanborn started collecting taxes that would have been paid anyway and pocketed half of that money, too.

When it became clear that Sanborn was living far beyond his means, a committee of Congress looked into the matter. Sanborn was removed from his position, and the committee recommended that Grant fire Richardson. Grant refused, but Richardson resigned on

SOURCE DOCUMENT

Grant was elected to a second term in 1873. Just as his second term began, more scandal and corruption surfaced. This is an invitation to Grant's second inaugural gala.

Ulysses S. Grant

his own. Grant gave Richardson's job to an honest Civil War veteran named Benjamin H. Bristow. Bristow is considered one of Grant's best appointments.

Not all the bad news in 1873 had to do with scandal. On September 18, a leading investment business named Jay Cooke & Company went bankrupt. It had been one of the nation's strongest banking houses since it was formed in 1861. Cooke had helped finance the Union's effort in the Civil War. After the war had ended, the company invested heavily in the building of new railroads, especially the Northern Pacific Railway.

With Cooke bankrupt, banks and other businesses with financial ties to Cooke also failed. People who worked for those companies suddenly lost their jobs. Those businesses that did not go bankrupt suffered financial losses, and their customers lost money. The term for an incident that causes widespread alarm in the financial world is "panic." This event became known as the Panic of 1873.

What caused the panic? There is no one answer. Some historians say it was too much growth too soon in the railroad industry. There were not enough investors, they say, to finance so much construction so fast.

Other historians argue that weak economies in Europe were caused in large part by a war between France and Prussia. Some experts say it had to do with the cost of rebuilding the city of Chicago, nearly destroyed by a disastrous fire in 1871. Still others believe it had to do with the many scandals of the Grant administration, which caused people to lose confidence in the government.

One success in Grant's second term came that fall. At that time, the Caribbean island of Cuba was ruled by Spain. Many Cuban natives wanted their home to be an independent country and were fighting Spanish rule. An armed ship called the *Virginius*, which was illegally flying the American flag, was being used by Cuban rebels to aid their conflict against Spain. On October 31, it was captured by the Spanish. A total of fifty-three crew members and passengers, including eight American citizens, were shot and killed.[7] Grant and Secretary of State Hamilton Fish demanded from Spain an apology and money to compensate for damages.

Some Americans called for war, but Grant and Fish believed war was not necessary. In early November, Spain apologized and agreed to pay eighty thousand dollars to be shared by the families of those who were executed.[8] War was avoided.

That was not the only good news late in 1873. The harsh criticism Congress took for the salary grab earlier in the year was still fresh in the lawmakers' minds. After returning to session in December, Congress repealed the back-pay raise for themselves.

But as 1873 turned into 1874, the economy was still sour, and American workers continued to suffer. Grant listened as his staff and Congress offered all kinds of advice. Business people felt the answer was to issue more paper money. But paper money needed to be backed up by a sufficient amount of gold. At first, Grant seemed to support that idea. As he considered it, though, he became concerned that such action would cause inflation, meaning prices would rise sharply and people could not afford needed goods and services.

On April 14, 1874, Congress passed what became known as the Inflation Bill. It called for $18 million in paper money to be added to the paper money already in circulation.[9] Although much of the American public supported the bill, Grant decided to veto it due to his concerns about high inflation. In doing so, Grant established a policy of keeping the nation's paper money supply tied into the gold supply. It would stay America's economic policy until the 1930s.

A lighter occasion dominated the news the next month. Ulysses and Julia Grant's daughter Nellie, who had grown from an awkward little girl into a charming young lady, was getting married. On May 21, Nellie appeared in a white satin dress in the East Room of the White House. To her side stood a young English singer named Algernon Sartoris. The two took their wedding vows under a huge arrangement of flowers in the shape of a bell. Grant, who did not often show outward emotion, cried in public as the wedding took place.[10]

Grant was as proud of his sons as he was of his daughter. Jesse was still a teenager, waiting to make his mark on the world. But Buck and Fred had grown into young men. Buck was a student at Harvard and Fred at West Point. The president did not expect his cadet son

SOURCE DOCUMENT

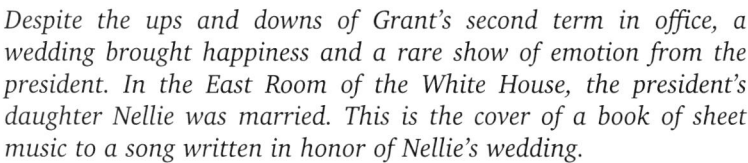

Despite the ups and downs of Grant's second term in office, a wedding brought happiness and a rare show of emotion from the president. In the East Room of the White House, the president's daughter Nellie was married. This is the cover of a book of sheet music to a song written in honor of Nellie's wedding.

to follow in his footsteps and become a career soldier, but he thought a West Point education was too valuable to pass up. The two older sons often spent summer breaks from their schooling visiting their father and mother at the Summer White House along the seashore in Long Branch, New Jersey. It was a favorite vacation spot where the Grants could escape muggy Washington summers.

During the summer and fall of 1874, the nation's economy continued to be weak. Several congressmen were up for reelection in November 1874. With many working people hurting, and public knowledge of so many scandals, the Democrats won huge victories in Congress. They controlled the House of Representatives for the first time since 1860.[11] Grant would have his hands full in dealing with Congress for his last two years in office.

8

"One Honest Man in St. Louis"

President Grant was now fifty-two years old. Less physically fit than in his youth and with several more pounds around his waist, he gave up his hobby of riding horses. Even so, he could not stay away from them. After finishing work for the day, he was often seen sitting in a carriage pulled by a pair of handsome horses down the streets of Washington.

The president and Julia were still devoted to one another. She loved being first lady, and her elegant gatherings became well known in the capital.[1] All classes of women were welcome at her fancy affairs. It did not matter if they were wealthy. A socialite named Benjamin Perley Poore wrote at the time that in attendance at White House galas were "ladies in diamonds, and others in dollar jewelry."[2]

Ulysses S. Grant

It was not unusual for Julia Grant to step beyond her duties as official White House hostess and offer the president a bit of advice concerning policy making. However, many historians say she was as naive as the president in judging people's characters.

Grant began 1875 on a positive note. A bill he supported was passed by Congress in January, and Grant signed it into law. It had to do with the economy and was called the Resumption of Specie Act. "Specie" is a term meaning "coined money." The bill stated that by January 1, 1879, the United States Treasury Department was required to keep enough gold in reserve so that all paper money could be redeemed for an equal amount of gold.

Then on March 1, he signed another bill into law. It was meant to protect African Americans from discrimination and became known as the Civil Rights Act of 1875. The law stated that all persons regardless of skin color will have "full and equal enjoyment" of public accommodations, including places of lodging, transportation, and theaters.[3] It was the last civil rights law passed by the United States Congress until 1957.[4]

Signing the Civil Rights Act was a brave political move for Grant since it angered white Southerners and killed any chance of attracting them to the Republican party. But as with previous similar acts, this law was very difficult to enforce. For example, in Yazoo City, Mississippi, in 1875, a group of white men attacked a group of African Americans, killing one, at an integrated

SOURCE DOCUMENT

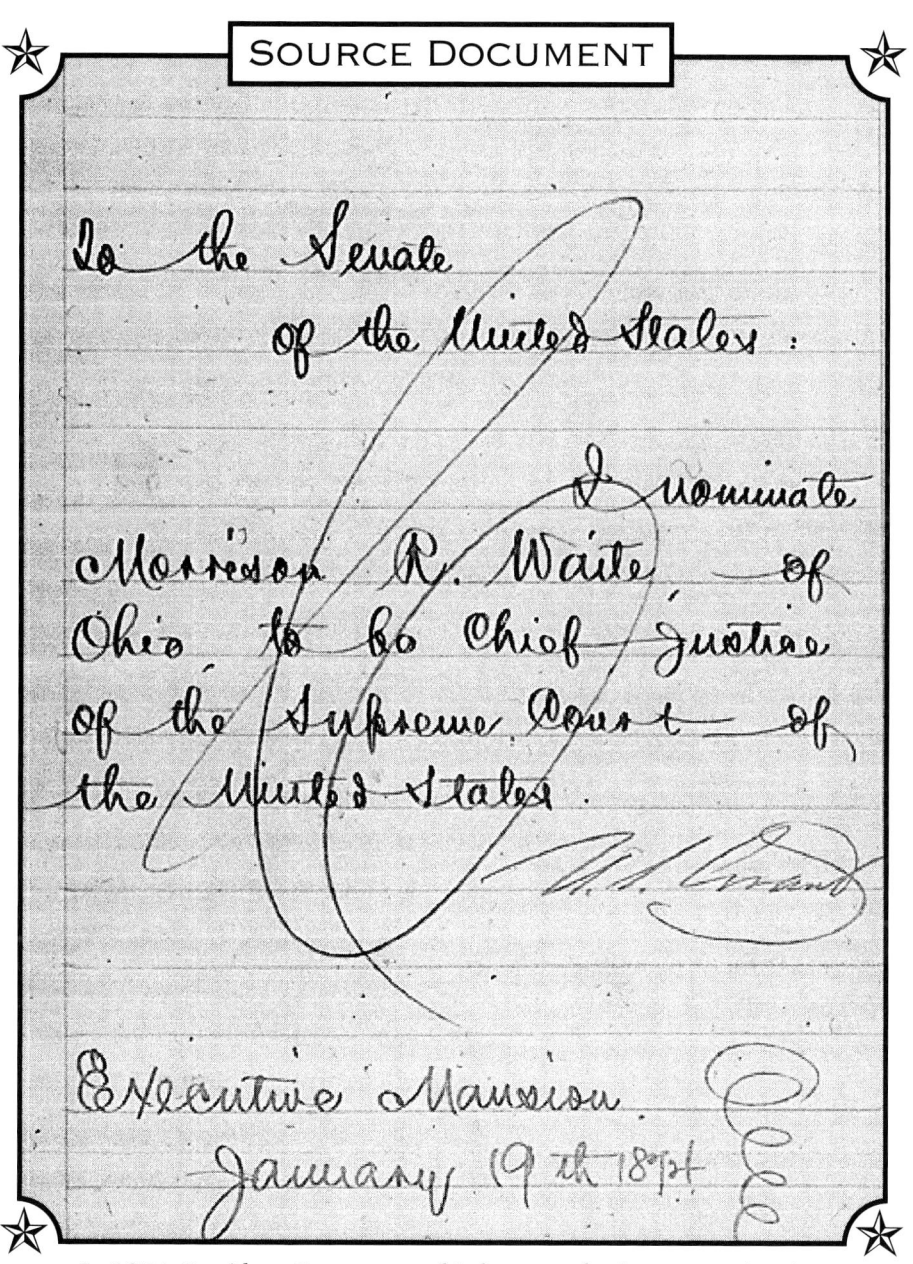

In 1874, President Grant wrote this letter to the Senate nominating Morrison R. Waite of Ohio to the United States Supreme Court.

political meeting. The assailants escaped out of town, and there were not enough police or federal troops to stop them or bring them to justice.

However, it was not long before scandal was in the news once more. Makers of alcohol were supposed to pay taxes to the federal government based on the amount they produced and distributed. It was the job of United States treasury agents to personally travel to each distillery and place a government stamp on each barrel of alcohol. The stamp meant the alcohol had been measured and a tax had been placed on it. It was then up to the whiskey distiller to honestly pay his taxes.

Some treasury agents came up with an idea to make money illegally. Whiskey distillers gave the agents money to keep personally. In return, the agents did not make them pay taxes on their products. Rumors of this illegal action had been floating around Washington for a while. Then Secretary of the Treasury Benjamin Bristow saw a list of the amount of liquor shipped from St. Louis. He compared those numbers with the total tax dollars collected. As Bristow suspected, the amount of taxes received was far short of the amount of money that should have been collected.

As soon as Bristow told Grant what he had discovered, the president assigned an investigator to get to the bottom of the scam. He was John McDonald, supervisor of the United States Internal Revenue Service Bureau in

"One Honest Man in St. Louis"

St. Louis. Grant said McDonald was the "one honest man in St. Louis on whom we can rely."[5]

Imagine Grant's disappointment to learn that McDonald was the ringleader of the whole crooked scheme, which became known as the Whiskey Ring. Then consider his disgust when he discovered that another person illegally taking money from the distillers was his old friend and personal secretary Orville E. Babcock.

To get physical evidence of wrongdoing, Bristow conducted a surprise raid on May 10, 1875. He sent men to sixteen distilleries in St. Louis, Chicago, and Milwaukee. They found overwhelming evidence of tax cheating. A total of 253 indictments, or official charges of breaking the law, were issued.[6] The investigations and trials of those alleged to have been involved made news throughout 1875, again reflecting poorly on Grant's leadership abilities.

Reconstruction in the South began to wind down around this time. It was difficult to try to enforce equal rights and protection of African Americans while at the same time welcoming the South back into the Union. Many living in the South were not ready to accept African Americans as equals. And many in the North continued to believe that the South should be harshly punished for seceding from the Union. Grant tried to satisfy both sides but was unable to satisfy either.

Taxes were high in the South, which hurt Northerners who conducted business with the former

Confederate states. The Ku Klux Klan and other white extremist groups continued to threaten African Americans to stop them from voting. Eventually, Southern white Democrats had been voted into local and state offices that had been held by Republicans for most of the prior ten years. These state legislatures passed laws that discriminated against African Americans. It seemed that Reconstruction policies had succeeded only in angering Southern whites, which stirred up even more bitterness between the races.[7]

Trials of those involved in the Whiskey Ring continued early into 1876. A total of 110 men were convicted.[8] According to Treasury secretary Benjamin Bristow, the government lost up to $15 million a year for several years because of tax cheaters involved in the scandal.[9] However, the majority of people who helped organize or were in charge of the scheme escaped punishment. That included Grant's friend Orville E. Babcock, who was found not guilty of all charges on February 28, 1876. Grant supported Babcock the entire time he was on trial.

Bristow was not so lucky. Treasury agents and other government workers found not guilty in the Whiskey Ring wanted revenge against Bristow for causing their troubles. They convinced Grant that Bristow's true goal was to disgrace the president for his own glory. Grant believed them, and under pressure from Grant, Bristow resigned his post. Americans of the day saw the Whiskey Ring as a sad comment on politics, as guilty people

"One Honest Man in St. Louis"

Julia Grant loved being first lady and often held fancy affairs that were attended by all classes of people. She would sometimes offer the president advice concerning policy making.

were set free and the courageous man who investigated the crime suffered by losing his job.

The Whiskey Ring was not the last scandal to take place under Grant. In 1876, Grant's last year in office, it was discovered that another person in a high position in Grant's administration took advantage of the president's trusting nature to satisfy his own greed.

William W. Belknap had been Grant's secretary of war since 1869. Belknap was a popular man with a winning manner. One part of his duties included appointing people to be in charge of trading posts in what was then called Indian Territory. This was land in the Far West that had not yet become states. Basically, the trading posts were stores where people in the army and American Indians who lived nearby could shop for items they needed.

The trading posts had very little competition, enabling the traders to charge whatever prices they wished. Through the help of his wife, Amanda, Belknap awarded a tradership to a family friend named Caleb

Marsh. To repay them for giving him the job, Marsh promised he would give the Belknaps a share of his profits.

Marsh was sent to the trading post at Fort Sill, Indian Territory. However, Fort Sill already had a person in charge, a man named John S. Evans. Upon arriving, Marsh explained to Evans that he had been chosen to take his place as head of the trading post. But Evans did not want to give up his job. Marsh said that was fine, but he wanted something in return for allowing Evans to stay at the post. So to satisfy Marsh, Evans made an agreement that he would pay Marsh twelve thousand dollars a year so he could keep his job.[10] Marsh, in turn, would pay half that money to Amanda Belknap. After Amanda's death, Marsh paid the money directly to Belknap.

Everyone but Evans, the person doing all the work, made extra money from this arrangement. Those who suffered most were local American Indians, who were forced to pay unfair high prices for goods they needed to survive.

This agreement went on for years until a member of the House of Representatives from Pennsylvania, Heister Clymer, was put in charge of making certain that money from the War Department was spent properly. By chance, Clymer and Belknap had been classmates in college. Clymer had heard rumors about illegal activities going on at Fort Sill. He investigated and uncovered the truth about the Belknaps, Marsh, and Evans.

"One Honest Man in St. Louis"

Clymer convinced Marsh to testify to the House of Representatives against Belknap.

On February 29, 1876, Marsh spilled the entire truth about the scheme to a special committee of the House of Representatives. Two days later, Clymer stood on the floor of the House of Representatives and demanded that his old college classmate be impeached. Belknap knew he was caught, and on the same day he resigned his post.

Even though Belknap was no longer secretary of war, the Senate held an impeachment trial against him. On August 1, 1876, a vote to impeach Belknap took place. The count was thirty-seven to convict and twenty-five to acquit.[11] As in any impeachment trial, two thirds of the vote was needed to convict. The total fell short of two thirds, but most senators who had voted to acquit admitted that Belknap was guilty. They did not think the Senate had a legal right to impeach a person no longer in office.[12]

As was usually the case, Grant expressed his full confidence in his troubled staff member. He did this even after the Senate trial had ended.[13]

As his presidency wound down, Grant was tired and seemed older than his fifty-four years. In his last message to Congress delivered on December 5, 1876, he confessed, "Mistakes have been made, as all can see and I admit."[14] He concluded his address by relating, ". . . I have acted in every instance from a conscientious desire to do what was right, constitutional within the law, and for the very best interests of the whole people. Failures have been errors of judgment, not of intent."[15]

The federal law at the time mandated that the president was to be inaugurated on March 4. However, in 1877, March 4 fell on a Sunday and President-elect Rutherford B. Hayes refused to be sworn in on the Christian Sabbath. Therefore, he was publicly inaugurated the next day, Monday, March 5.

What the American people did not know is that Hayes, Grant, and Chief Justice of the United States Supreme Court Morrison R. Waite met at the White House the evening of Saturday, March 3. Just before dinner was served, the three men along with several witnesses entered the Red Room of the White House where Hayes was secretly and officially sworn in as President of the United States—two days before he went through the formality of an inauguration ceremony in public. It was clear that Grant was ready to leave his post.

Grant later declared, "I never wanted to get out of a place as much as I did to get out of the presidency."[16]

9

". . . How I Can Ever Trust Any Human Being Again"

Grant got his wish to leave the White House. On March 5, 1877, Rutherford B. Hayes was sworn in as president, and Ulysses S. Grant became a private citizen once again.

Only fifty-four years old, he had already been a war hero and served two terms as president. In contrast, Thomas Jefferson was not even elected president until he was fifty-seven. Harry Truman was sixty when he became president, and Ronald Reagan was sixty-nine when he was sworn into office.

Grant had always enjoyed traveling but had never been overseas. So he and Julia decided to take a long vacation and see the world. Grant had never been a rich man, but he was able to finance his trip with eighty-five thousand dollars he had earned from successful investments.[1] On May 17, 1877, the former president and first lady and their nineteen-year-old son Jesse set sail from Philadelphia on a passenger steamer named *Indiana*. Crossing the Atlantic Ocean was tough for Julia, who got seasick. The former president, however, felt fine and enjoyed numerous cigars every day. On May 28, *Indiana* docked in Liverpool, England.

No one who spent any time with Grant in England would have had any idea that he was unpopular at home. The British people loved him. To them he was the son of a simple tanner who became president of the United States and was one of the greatest war heroes on earth.

Queen Victoria invited the Grants to dinner at her home at Windsor Castle on June 26. Their son Jesse did not receive an invitation. A diplomat asked the queen on behalf of the Grants if Jesse could be invited as well. The request was granted.

However, Jesse learned he would not be seated at the queen's table but placed in another room with the household staff. Jesse was outraged and said he refused to eat with servants.

The queen's staff tried to assure Jesse that sitting in a different room was not an insult. One of Queen Victoria's ladies-in-waiting, or personal attendants, assured Jesse that she would be in the same dining room as he, and she was hardly an uneducated servant.

". . . How I Can Ever Trust Any Human Being Again"

At only fifty-four years old, Ulysses S. Grant was again a private citizen after serving two terms as president. Grant, Julia, and their son Jesse went on a much needed vacation. In June 1877, Grant and his family met Queen Victoria at Windsor Castle in England.

But that was not good enough for Jesse. He angrily said that if he could not sit at the queen's table, he would go back to his hotel room.

The master of the queen's household, Sir John Cowell, pleaded with Jesse not to leave. It would be embarrassing to the queen. The former president defended his son. Finally, the queen announced through Cowell that she would be very happy to have Jesse dine with her at her table. So they all ate together.

At one point during the dinner, Julia made a comment that became famous. When the queen told the former first lady about all the wearisome duties she had to fulfill, Julia responded, "Yes, I can imagine them; I, too have been the wife of a great ruler."[2] As for Jesse, the queen made friendly conversation with him. However, she was not impressed. She later referred to him as "a very ill-mannered young Yankee."[3]

From England, the Grants traveled to Scotland, Belgium, and France. The former leader appeared able to forget about politics. In a letter he wrote in Paris on October 25, 1877, to his brother-in-law, Grant said, "I keep very little track of political matters at home" and, "I have not yet experienced any discomfort from lack of employment after sixteen years of continuous care and responsibilities."[4]

Everywhere the Grants traveled they were treated as celebrities. Even though their goals were to see the wonderful sights of the world, to the residents of other countries the Grants were the sights to be seen.

After Europe, they journeyed through the Middle East and Asia. In China, General Li Hung Chang told his guest, "You and I, General Grant, are the greatest men in the world."[5] The Grant family was then treated to a state banquet consisting of seventy courses.[6]

After nearly two and a half years roaming the world, the Grants decided that it was time to head home. Grant had mixed feelings. He wrote, "I am both homesick and dread going home."[7] They sailed into San Francisco on September 20, 1879.

As it turned out, Grant had nothing to fear. He was welcomed home with a burst of enthusiasm. But before

". . . How I Can Ever Trust Any Human Being Again"

settling down, the Grants had another trip to take. Ever since his days in the Mexican War, Grant had a love for Hispanic people, so he and Julia spent some time touring Cuba, the West Indies, and Mexico. They then moved back to Galena, Illinois, into the house the townspeople had awarded him fifteen years earlier.

In June 1880, the Republicans held their convention in Chicago. Rutherford B. Hayes chose not to run for a second term. The Republicans' first choice to succeed Hayes was none other than former president Grant. Grant's supporters believed the fifty-eight-year-old war hero had learned from his mistakes. While Grant publicly did not express enthusiasm about being nominated again, he never declared he was not a candidate. Some historians believe that with the knowledge he obtained through his world travels, Grant believed he was more qualified than ever to serve as president.[8]

On the first ballot, Grant led with 304 delegates' votes. His closest opponent was Representative James G. Blaine of Maine with 284.[9] Since no person had the needed 378 ballots, the delegates kept voting.

Grant led on the first thirty-five ballots. But he never had enough votes to be nominated.[10] Finally, on the thirty-sixth ballot, a compromise candidate, Ohio congressman James A. Garfield, was chosen. He went on to be elected president in November.

In 1881, Grant took another trip to Mexico. The purpose this time was to conduct business. Grant had been named president of the new Mexican Southern

SOURCE DOCUMENT

No. 62.   2 pp.

Gen. Grant's Reasons for Supporting Gen. Garfield.

A SHARPLY-DRAWN CONTRAST.

SPEECH AT WARREN, O., SEPT. 28, 1880.

In view of the known character and ability of the speaker who is to address you to-day, and his long public career and association with the leading statesmen of this country for the past twenty years, it would not be becoming in me to detain you with many remarks of my own. But it might be proper for me to account to you, on the first occasion of my presiding at political meetings, for the faith that is in me.

I am a republican, as the two great political parties are now divided, because the republican party is a national party, seeking the greatest good for the greatest number of citizens. There is not a precinct in this vast nation where a democrat cannot cast his ballot and have it counted as cast. No matter what the prominence of the opposite party, he can proclaim his political opinions, even if he is only one among a thousand, without fear and without proscription on account of his opinions. There are fourteen states, and localities in other states, where republicans have not this privilege. This is one reason why I am a republican. But I am a republican for many other reasons.

The republican party assures protection to life and property, the public credit and the payment of the debts of the government, state, county or municipality so far as it can control. The democratic party does not promise this; if it does, it has broken its promises to the extent of hundreds of millions, as many northern democrats can testify to their sorrow.

I am a republican as between existing parties, because it fosters the productions of the field and farm, and of manufactories, and it encourages general education of the poor as well as the rich. The democratic party discourages all these where in absolute power.

The republican party is a party of progress and of liberality toward its opponents. It encourages the poor to strive to better their condition, the ignorant to educate their children to enable them to compete successfully with their more fortunate associates; and, in fine, it secures an entire equality before the law of every citizen, no matter what his race, nationality or previous condition.

It tolerates no privileged class. Every one has the opportunity to make himself all he is capable of.

Ladies and gentlemen, do you believe this can be truthfully said in the greater part of fourteen of the states of this union to-day, which the democratic party control absolutely?

The republican party is a party of principles—the same principles prevailing wherever it has a foothold.

The democratic party is united on but one thing, and that is in getting control of the government in all its branches. It is for internal improvement at the expense of the government in one section, and against this in another. It favors repudiation of solemn obligations in one section and honest payment of debts in another (where public opinion will not tolerate any other view.) It favors fiat money in one place and good money in another. Finally, it favors the pooling of all issues not favored by the republicans, to the end that it may secure the one principle upon which the party is a most harmonious unit, namely, gaining control of the government in all its branches.

I have been in some part of every state lately in rebellion within the last year. I was most hospitably received at every place where I stopped. My receptions were not by the Union class alone, but by all classes without distinction. I had free talk with many who were against us in the war, and who have been against the republican party ever since. They were in all instances reasonable men, judged by what they said. I believed then, and believe now, that they sincerely want a break-up in this solid-south political condition. They see that it is to their pecuniary interests as well as to their happiness that there should be harmony and confidence between all sections. They want to break away from the slavery which binds them to a party

By 1880, Grant was back home in Galena, Illinois. That election year, President Rutherford B. Hayes chose not to run again. Some Republicans wanted Grant to run for president. Grant never received enough votes to earn his party's nomination, so a compromise candidate was chosen—James A. Garfield. Grant gave his reasons for supporting Garfield in the above document from 1880.

". . . How I Can Ever Trust Any Human Being Again"

Railroad. Its goal was to build a railroad from Mexico City south to the Guatemala border.

Since the Mexican Southern Railroad had its American office in New York City, Grant moved east from Illinois to be near it. Grant's title, however, was mainly an honorary one. He had few hands-on roles in the company's business. It did not matter, since the railroad project never panned out. So Grant looked for something else to do with the rest of his life.

The nation suffered a tragedy in July 1881 when President Garfield was shot. He lingered for several weeks but died that September. Vice President Chester A. Arthur became president. President Arthur chose Grant and a former Confederate official named William H. Trescot to travel to Mexico City to negotiate a trade agreement between the two countries. They were successful, agreeing with Mexico to import varied products and manufactured items into each nation without any tariffs. The pact was signed in January 1883. But for political reasons, Congress never made it law. Senators wanting to keep tariffs high to protect American products killed it.

That was the last of Grant's work in politics. He then decided to make his mark as a businessman. But Grant was no better a judge of people's honesty as a private citizen than he was as a politician. In many ways, he was still like Lyss Grant, the little boy who bungled the colt sale so many years ago.

Grant's son, Ulysses, Jr., or Buck, was by now a

grown man. Buck Grant opened a banking firm in New York City's financial district with another man named Ferdinand Ward. The job of the new company, Grant & Ward, was to invest other people's money in new businesses and other ventures. The retired president thought Grant & Ward was a promising firm. Ward had a reputation as a real go-getter in the financial world. So Ward convinced Grant to invest his life savings in his company.

However, Buck Grant inherited his father's poor business sense. Ward was a risk taker and not always honest with his customers. On May 4, 1884, Ward told the general and his son horrible news. The bank where Grant and Ward kept their company's money was almost bankrupt. Today there are laws that protect money people deposit in banks. There were no such laws in 1884.

Ward told Grant to borrow enough money to keep the bank in business a little longer. Grant sought out one of the richest men in the world, William H. Vanderbilt. Vanderbilt's grandfather had made a huge fortune in the railroad industry.

Like a small child begging his father for a raise in his allowance, the former president of the United States pleaded with Vanderbilt for a loan. Vanderbilt offered Grant one hundred and fifty thousand dollars. Grant took the money, but he was humiliated to have to do so.[11]

Vanderbilt's loan did not help. The bank failed on

". . . How I Can Ever Trust Any Human Being Again"

May 7. All who had invested money in Grant & Ward lost every penny they had. That included both Grants.

Ferdinand Ward was later convicted of grand larceny and sentenced to ten years in prison. But that was little comfort to the penniless Grant family. Grant said sadly, "I have made it a rule of my life to trust a man long after other people gave him up, but I don't see how I can ever trust any human being again."[12] Grant's life was to turn even more tragic. In the summer of 1884, the former president bit into a peach and felt a horrible pain in his mouth. A doctor discovered that he had throat cancer, most likely caused by years of smoking as many as twenty cigars a day. Grant was told the disease was fatal.

He had always cared about his family and wanted them to be financially secure after he died. What could a man in poor health do to earn money fast? For a former general and president, the answer was simple. He would write the story of his life. It would be published as a book and his surviving family members would get any money earned from its sales after his death.

In February 1885, Grant signed a contract with author Mark Twain to publish his life story. Grant knew by then that he did not have long to live. So he began putting words on paper as fast as he could. During the Civil War, Grant had fought against some of the strongest armies ever formed. Now he had to win one final battle, against time.

As his body weakened, Grant plugged on through

SOURCE DOCUMENT

TO THE SENATE OF THE UNITED STATES:

I NOMINATE Ulysses S. Grant, formerly General Commanding the Armies of the United States, to be General on the Retired List of the Army, with the full pay of such rank.

Chester A. Arthur

EXECUTIVE MANSION,
WASHINGTON, March 3d, 1885

President Chester A. Arthur addressed this letter to the Senate in 1885, nominating Ulysses S. Grant to be general on the retired list.

"... How I Can Ever Trust Any Human Being Again"

the spring. But summer was approaching, and with it the torrid and stagnant city heat. This was decades before air conditioning was invented. It was believed at the time that cool mountain air was good for one's health.

A friend named Joseph Drexel offered Grant the use of his roomy cottage perched atop Mount McGregor on the outskirts of the town of Wilton, New York. Wilton is located just outside the fashionable resort town of Saratoga Springs and about 180 miles north of New

After Ulysses S. Grant was diagnosed with throat cancer in 1884, he retreated to this cottage in Wilton, New York, to relax and to write his memoirs.

Ulysses S. Grant

Wanting his family to be secure after his death, Grant wrote his memoirs with what strength he had and finished his book July 11, 1885. Just days later, on July 23, Ulysses S. Grant died.

". . . How I Can Ever Trust Any Human Being Again"

York City. Grant accepted the offer and arrived at the cottage on June 26, 1885. For years, people from New York City, the Midwest, and the South had journeyed to Saratoga to enjoy bathing in its natural springs.

But to Grant, the tourists delighting in the nearby waters could have been a million miles away. He was in a frantic race against time. For his family to be secure after his death, he had to complete his life story. He was in horrible pain. His throat hurt so much that he could barely speak. The pain was so great that he could not lie down. He slept at night while sitting upright in an upholstered easy chair, extending his legs onto another chair facing him. In the daytime, he continued to write, and write, and write.

On July 11, 1885, Grant finished his book. On July 20, he mustered whatever strength he could to walk outdoors. The tanner's son who grew to become one of the world's most respected citizens stood on a ledge and took in the inspiring view of the valley below, where people were living life to the fullest in beautiful Saratoga. Three days later, Ulysses S. Grant surrendered in his final battle as he breathed his last breath.

But he had won his battle against time. The book was a huge success and is considered one of the best military memoirs ever written.

Grant's funeral was fit for a fallen hero and statesman. His body lay in state in Albany, New York, then in New York City. Following a solemn but grand service, Grant was buried on the Upper West Side of Manhattan

Ulysses S. Grant

General Grant National Memorial in New York City is the largest mausoleum in North America.

on August 8, 1885. It is estimated that sixty thousand people marched in his funeral service.[13]

Twelve years later, a massive structure of granite and white marble was built over Grant's burial site. Today it is officially called General Grant National Memorial, but most people casually refer to it as Grant's Tomb. It is the largest mausoleum, or single tomb, in North America.[14]

10

Legacy

Presidential historians each have different areas in which they are experts. Like all people, they also have varied political views. Despite this, they have one thing in common. Nearly every one says that Ulysses S. Grant was one of the worst presidents in the history of the United States.

Over the years, several surveys ranking the presidents have been taken. One of the first was conducted in 1948 by writer Arthur Schlesinger, who surveyed fifty-five historians. Out of twenty-nine presidents ranked, Grant finished twenty-eighth. Only Warren G. Harding finished lower.[1] Many similar polls have been taken from 1962 through 1997. In each poll, Grant was ranked either below average or a failure.[2]

Ulysses S. Grant

Why is he viewed as such a poor president? The main answer can be summed up in one word: corruption. Authors William J. Ridings, Jr., and Stuart B. McIver wrote in 1997 a book called *Rating the Presidents*, based on a poll they conducted. The authors said, "Though honest himself, Grant misplaced his trust in many dishonest friends."[3] Historian Richard E. Neustadt added, "Once he placed trust in a man, he tended loyally to keep that man for longer than any president should."[4]

But that is not all. Several historians blame Grant for being unable to make Reconstruction work. Because of that, they say, African Americans suffered legalized discrimination in the South for roughly ninety years until the civil rights movement of the 1960s. While author William S. McFeely credited Grant for signing the Ku Klux Klan Act and other civil rights laws, he wrote,

> When skillful racists organized opposition to blacks, Grant did not find a way to make the laws effective. He could have sent scores of government lawyers south as United States district attorneys under the direction of the Justice Department. He could have established a vastly strengthened constabulary [or armed police force] of United States marshals; instead, he did nothing until he was forced to send troops because local violence had reached crisis proportions.[5]

Yet there are those who defend Grant's presidency. They fault the United States Supreme Court for helping kill Reconstruction. In 1881, the Supreme Court overturned the Ku Klux Klan Act. Then two years later, it

SOURCE DOCUMENT

Published by Chs Magnus 12 Frankfort St. N.Y.

OUR ULYSSES.

By JOHN ROSS DIX.

Air: The Groves of Blarney.

A new Song this is of the great Ulysses,
  Who leads on our armies so great and grand;—
To the admiration of all the Nation,
  He's fighting for Peace in our native land!
We've Generals so many, but there isn't any
  That like General Grant can turn the flanks
Of the stubborn Rebels, and rout the devils,
  And their Jeff Davis's ragged ranks!

Fort Donelson's story proclaims his glory,—
  And Vicksburgh before him had to fall;
The foe at Shiloh, he compelled to lie low,
  And the Wilderness echoed his cannon ball!
He caused emotion, with the great explosion,
  When Petersburg Rebels his prowess saw;
Now, with Richmond before him, and our bright flag o'er him,
  For Freedom and Union still his sword he'll draw!

He's no great talker—but an awful balker
  Of the deep laid schemings of General Lee;
And if there is any one, can end this Rebellion,
  Sure Ulysses Grant must that soldier be!
Then hurrah! for the General, and cheers for his men who're al
  Determined never to retire or yield,
Whatsoe'er befalls him, while his Country calls him,
  Or a single Rebel shall contest the field!

Entered according to Act of Congress, in the year 1864, by CHARLES MAGNUS, in the Clerk's Office of the District Court of the United States for the Southern District of New York.

500 Illustrated Ballads, lithographed and printed by
CHARLES MAGNUS, No. 12 Frankfort Street, New York.
Branch Office: No. 520 7th St., Washington, D. C.

This song was written in honor of the general who was still fighting in the Civil War. Ulysses S. Grant went from a war hero, to president for two terms, to elder statesman, and finally to author of what is considered one of the best military memoirs ever written.

overturned the Civil Rights Act of 1875, which Grant had bravely signed.

One who stands by Grant's record is history professor John Y. Simon of Southern Illinois University, Carbondale. Simon had made it his life's project to collect and publish all Grant's letters and presidential papers. According to Simon, several younger historians who came of age during the civil rights movement in the 1960s see Grant as a hero for defending African Americans' rights when it was a risky thing to do.

Simon states that many of Grant's policies regarding race did work. He credits the laws Grant signed for the death of the Ku Klux Klan of the Reconstruction era. (However, a new Ku Klux Klan exists today.)

As far as the corruption, Grant handled it as best as he could, reports Simon. He concedes that some of Grant's staff, such as Orville Babcock, did take advantage of Grant's trusting nature. But Simon insists that it is important to remember that once Grant caught on to Jay Gould and James Fisk's scheme, he immediately did the right thing by ordering the United States Treasury to sell gold supplies. Simon remarks, "If Grant really left the office in disgrace, why was there a push to put him to serve a third term."[6]

Simon also notes, "Grant gets best marks for keeping the peace. There was provocation from Great Britain and Spain over the *Alabama* [and the other warships] and the *Virginius*. Grant avoided war, although many

Legacy

called for war. That is not mentioned by [older] historians."[7]

Simon sums up his views by adding, "Grant wasn't the best but he wasn't the worst. I would put him in the average category, more like John Quincy Adams. Grant is rising in the polls."[8]

Will Grant be seen in a more positive light as younger historians take more important positions? Only time will tell.

"DEATH OF GENERAL GRANT"

As one by one withdraw the lofty actors,

From that great play on history's stage eterne,

That lurid, partial act of war and peace—of old and new contending,

Fought out through wrath, fears, dark dismays, and many a long suspense;

All past—and since, in countless graves receding, mellowing,

Victor's and vanquish'd—Lincoln's and Lee's—now thou with them,

Man of the mighty days—and equal to the days!

Thou from the prairies!—tangled and many-vein'd and hard has been thy part,

To admiration has it been enacted!

—Walt Whitman 1885

Chronology

1822—Born Hiram Ulysses Grant in Point Pleasant, Ohio, on April 27 to Jesse and Hannah Simpson Grant.

1823—Moves with family to Georgetown, Ohio.

1839—Begins education at United States Military Academy at West Point, New York; becomes known by new name, Ulysses S. Grant.

1843—Graduates West Point ranked in middle of class; is stationed at Jefferson Barracks, St. Louis, Missouri.

1844—Transferred to Camp Salubrity, Louisiana.

1846–1847—Fights in Mexican War.

1848—Marries Julia Dent on August 22.

1848–1852—Stationed various times in Detroit, Michigan, and Sackets Harbor, New York.

1850—Son Frederick Dent Grant is born.

1852—Transferred to Fort Vancouver, Washington Territory, where he begins drinking; son Ulysses S. (Buck) Grant, Jr., is born.

1854—Transferred to Fort Humboldt, California; resigns from United States Army.

1855—Begins farming career in St. Louis; daughter Ellen Wrenshall (Nellie) Grant is born.

1858—Son Jesse Root Grant is born; quits farming career; begins odd jobs.

1860—Moves to Galena, Illinois, to work in father's tannery.

Ulysses S. Grant

1861—Volunteers for United States Army as Civil War begins; named brigadier general; leads Union troops to victory at Belmont, Missouri.

1862—Victories in Tennessee at Fort Henry, Fort Donelson, and Shiloh.

1863—Siege, then victory in Vicksburg, Mississippi; major victory in Chattanooga, Tennessee.

1864—Awarded rank of lieutenant general; siege of Petersburg begins.

1865—Victory in Petersburg; accepts Lee's surrender at Appomattox Court House, Virginia; spends much of year accepting honors on tour of United States.

1866—Awarded rank of full general.

1867—Named secretary of war by President Andrew Johnson, then defies Johnson by stepping down from post.

1868—Elected president of United States.

1869—Attempts annexation of Santo Domingo; gold market scandal and Black Friday.

1870—Fifteenth Amendment to United States Constitution ratified; Enforcement Act passed; Santo Domingo annexation defeated.

1871—Ku Klux Klan Act passed; Treaty of Washington approved.

1872—Credit Mobilier scandal; reelected to second term as president; salary grab scandal begins.

1873—Richardson–Sanborn scandal; Panic of 1873 begins; *Virginius* affair occurs; Congress repeals back-pay raise.

1874—Vetoes Inflation bill; daughter Nellie Grant

Chronology

marries in White House; Democrats sweep to victory in congressional elections.

1875—Signs Resumption of Specie Act; Whiskey Ring scandal becomes public.

1876—Belknap trading post scandal exposed.

1877—Administration ends as Rutherford B. Hayes sworn in as president on March 5.

1877–1879—Tours much of the world with family.

1880—Settles in Galena, Illinois; runs for third presidential term, but loses nomination to James A. Garfield.

1881—Named president of Mexican Southern Railroad; moves to New York City.

1882—Helps negotiate business agreement with Mexico.

1884—Loses life's savings in unwise investments.

1885—Write memoirs; dies on July 23.

1902—Julia Grant dies.

Did You Know?
Trivia from the President's lifetime

Did you know that the favorite Christmas poem, "T'was the night before Christmas," was written by Clement Moore in 1822, the year Ulysses S. Grant was born?

Did you know that in 1846 the first recorded baseball game was played? The setting was Elysian Field in Hoboken, New Jersey, and the New York Nine beat the Knickerbockers 23 to 1.

Did you know in 1858 a man named Hyman Lipman patented a new invention: a pencil with an eraser attached to the top?

Did you know that in 1865 French science fiction author Jules Verne wrote *From the Earth to the Moon*, in which he predicted that the United States would lead the world in space exploration?

Did you know in the early 1870s the most popular participatory sport among young people in the United States was roller skating?

Did you know that in 1885 the country's first self-service restaurant opened in New York City?

Chapter Notes

Chapter 2. The Tanner's Son

1. Jean Edward Smith, *Grant* (New York: Simon & Schuster, 2001), p. 22.
2. Personal interview with Pam Sanfilippo, January 10, 2002.
3. Ibid.
4. Brooks D. Simpson, *Ulysses S. Grant: Triumph over Adversity 1822–1865* (Boston, Mass.: Houghton Mifflin Company, 2000), p. 6.
5. Ulysses S. Grant, Caleb Carr series editor, *Personal Memoirs* (New York: The Modern Library, 1999), p. 10.
6. Ibid.
7. Ibid.
8. Personal interview with Judy Ruthven, January 12, 2002.
9. Grant, p. 8.
10. Smith, p. 23.
11. John Y. Simon, *The Papers of Ulysses S. Grant, Volume 1: 1837–1861* (Carbondale, Ill.: Southern Illinois University Press, 1967), p. 5.
12. Personal interview with Dr. Stephen Grove, January 10, 2002.
13. Ibid.
14. Grant, p. 18.
15. Personal interview with Pam Sanfilippo, January 10, 2002.
16. Grant, pp. 17–18.

Chapter 3. Crossing the Creek

1. Personal interview with Pam Sanfilippo, January 23, 2002.
2. John Y. Simon, *The Papers of Ulysses S. Grant, Volume 1: 1837–1861* (Carbondale, Ill.: Southern Illinois University Press, 1967), p. 25.
3. Brooks D. Simpson, *Ulysses S. Grant: Triumph over Adversity 1822–1865* (Boston, Mass.: Houghton Mifflin Company, 2000), p. 25.
4. Simon, p. 83.
5. Ulysses S. Grant, Caleb Carr series editor, *Personal Memoirs* (New York: The Modern Library, 1999), p. 45.
6. Simon, p. 142.
7. Simpson, p. 40.
8. Grant, p. 23.

9. *The Civil War*, episode 6, produced by Ken Burns and Ric Burns, production of Florentine Films, first broadcast on PBS network, 1989.

10. Personal interview with Pam Sanfilippo, January 23, 2002.

11. Simon, p. 316.

12. Ibid., p. 327.

13. Albert D. Richardson, *Personal History of Ulysses S. Grant* (Hartford, Conn.: American Publishing, 1868), p. 149, as quoted in Simpson, p. 62.

14. Simpson, p. 67.

Chapter 4. "He *Fights*"

1. W. E. Woodward, *Meet General Grant* (New York: Liveright Books, 1946, 1965), p. 178.

2. Robert Paul Jordan, *The Civil War* (Washington, D.C.: National Geographic Society, 1969), p. 83.

3. Ulysses S. Grant, Caleb Carr series editor, *Personal Memoirs* (New York: The Modern Library, 1999), p. 187.

4. Jordan, p. 83.

5. *The Civil War*, episode 2, produced by Ken Burns and Ric Burns, production of Florentine Films, first broadcast on PBS network, 1989.

6. Ibid., episode 6.

7. Jean Edward Smith, *Grant* (New York: Simon & Schuster, 2001), p. 225.

8. Jerry Korn, *War on the Mississippi: Grant's Vicksburg Campaign* (Alexandria, Va.: Time-Life Books, 1985), p. 58.

9. Jordan, p. 159.

10. *The Civil War*, episode 6.

11. Bruce Catton, *Grant Takes Command* (Boston: Little, Brown, 1968), p. 68.

Chapter 5. "Let Us Have Peace"

1. Jim Bishop, *The Day Lincoln Was Shot* (New York: Harper & Brothers, 1955), p. 113.

2. William J. Ridings, Jr. and Stuart B. McGiver, *Rating the Presidents* (Secaucus, N.J.: Citadel Press, 1997), p. 115.

3. Ibid., p. 116.

4. Personal interview with Jim Small, January 29, 2002.

5. W. E. Woodward, *Meet General Grant* (New York: Liveright Books, 1946, 1965), p. 367.

6. Personal interview with Jim Small, January 29, 2002.

7. Ibid.

Chapter Notes

8. William A. DeGregorio, *The Complete Book of U.S. Presidents* (New York: Wings Books, 1991), p. 254.

9. William B. Hesseltine, *Ulysses S. Grant: Politician* (New York, 1935), p. 127, as quoted in Paul F. Boller, Jr., *Presidential Campaigns* (New York: Oxford University Press, 1985), p. 124.

10. Boller, p. 125.

Chapter 6. No King Midas

1. David C. Whitney, *The American Presidents* (Garden City, N.Y.: Doubleday & Company, Inc., 1978), p. 162.

2. W. E. Woodward, *Meet General Grant* (New York: Liveright Books, 1946, 1965), p. 445.

3. William S. McFeely, *Grant: A Biography* (New York: W.W. Norton & Company, 1981), p. 341.

4. John W. Forney to Orville E. Babcock, February 28, 1970, Babcock Papers, Newberry Library, Chicago, as quoted in McFeely, p. 341.

5. Nathan Miller, *Star-Spangled Men: America's Ten Worst Presidents* (New York: A Lisa DrewBook/Scribner, 1998), p. 123.

6. Brooks D. Simpson, *The Reconstruction Presidents* (Lawrence, Kan.: University Press of Kansas, 1998), p. 150.

7. Woodward, p. 450.

8. "U. S. Grant Chronology," n.d. <http://www.lib.siu.edu/projects/usgrant/grant2.htm>, (February 1, 2002).

9. John A. Carpenter, *Ulysses S. Grant* (New York: Twayne Publishers, Inc., 1970), p. 110.

10. "Interview: William Crook," material taken from "William Crook, Through Five Administrations," n.d. <http://www.mscomm.com/~ulysses/page25.html> (January 30, 2002).

11. Ibid.

Chapter 7. A Victory, a Panic, and a Wedding

1. Paul F. Boller, Jr., *Presidential Campaigns* (New York: Oxford University Press, 1985), p. 128.

2. Eugene H. Roseboom, *A History of Presidential Elections* (New York: Macmillian, 1957), p. 231.

3. Nathan Miller, *Star-Spangled Men: America's Ten Worst Presidents* (New York: A Lisa DrewBook/Scribner, 1998), p. 124.

4. David C. Whitney, *The American Presidents* (Garden City, N.Y.: Doubleday & Company, Inc., 1978), p. 401.

5. John A. Carpenter, *Ulysses S. Grant* (New York: Twayne Publishers, Inc., 1970), p. 128.

6. W. E. Woodward, *Meet General Grant* (New York: Liveright Books, 1946, 1965), p. 418.

Ulysses S. Grant

7. Carpenter, p. 134.

8. "The Virginius Affair," The Columbia Encyclopedia, Sixth Edition, 2001, <http://www.bartleby.com/65/vi/Virginiu.html> (February 13, 2002).

9. Woodward, p. 453.

10. Lonnelle Aikman, *The Living White House* (Washington, D.C.: National Geographic Society, Special Publications Division, 1967), p. 48.

11. Carpenter, p. 135.

Chapter 8. "One Honest Man in St. Louis"

1. Paul E. Boller, Jr., *Presidential Wives* (New York: Oxford University Press, 1988), p. 134.

2. Ishbel Ross, *The General's Wife: The Life of Mrs. Ulysses S. Grant* (New York, 1959), p. 204, as quoted in Boller.

3. National Civil Rights Museum, n.d. <www.civilrightsmuseum.org> (February 1, 2002).

4. Ibid.

5. William J. Ridings, Jr. and Stuart B. McGiver, *Rating the Presidents* (Secaucus, N.J.: Citadel Press, 1997), p. 125.

6. W. E. Woodward, *Meet General Grant* (New York: Liveright Books, 1946, 1965), p. 421.

7. Ridings, p. 125.

8. William A. DeGregorio, *The Complete Book of U.S. Presidents* (New York: Wings Books, 1991), p. 271.

9. Ridings, p. 125.

10. Woodward, p. 425.

11. John A. Carpenter, *Ulysses S. Grant* (New York: Twayne Publishers, Inc., 1970), p. 157.

12. Woodward, p. 426.

13. Carpenter, p. 157.

14. "Ulysses S. Grant Chronology," n.d. <www.lib.siu.edu/projects/usgrant/grant2.htm> (February 1, 2002).

15. Ibid.

16. *The American Presidents*, "The Heroic Posture" episode, co-production of Kunhardt Productions and Thirteen/WNET, Kunhardt Productions, first broadcast on PBS network, 2000.

Chapter 9. ". . . How I Can Ever Trust Any Human Being Again"

1. Jean Edward Smith, *Grant* (New York: Simon & Schuster, 2001), p. 607.

2. Adam Babeau, *Grant in Peace* (Freeport, N.Y.: 1887, 1971),

Chapter Notes

p. 288, as quoted in Paul E. Boller, Jr., *Presidential Wives* (New York: Oxford University Press, 1988), p. 144.

3. William S. McFeely, *Grant: A Biography* (New York: W.W. Norton & Company, 1981), p. 459.

4. Jess Grant Cramer, *Letters of Ulysses S. Grant to his Father and his Youngest Sister, 1857–78* (New York: G. P. Putnam's Sons, 1912), pp. 135–136.

5. McFeely, p. 472.

6. W. E. Woodward, *Meet General Grant* (New York: Liveright Books, 1946, 1965), p. 474.

7. Kenneth W. Leish, Editor in Charge, *The American Heritage Pictorial History of the Presidents of the United States*, volume 1 (New York: American Heritage Publishing Co., Inc., 1968), p. 482.

8. Smith, pp. 614–615.

9. Woodward, p. 475.

10. William A. DeGregorio, *The Complete Book of U.S. Presidents* (New York: Wings Books, 1991), p. 273.

11. Woodward, p. 487.

12. David C. Whitney, *The American Presidents* (Garden City, N.Y.: Doubleday & Company, Inc., 1978), p. 164.

13. Brian Lamb and the C-SPAN staff, *Who's Buried in Grant's Tomb?* (Washington, D.C.: National Cable Satellite Corporation, 2000), p. 76.

14. Ibid.

Chapter 10. Legacy

1. Robert K. Murray and Tim H. Blessing, "The Presidential Performance Study: A Progress Report," *The Journal of American History*, December 1983, p. 541.

2. Ibid., pp. 540–541, and William J. Ridings, Jr., and Stuart B. McGiver, *Rating the Presidents* (Secaucus, N.J.: Citadel Press, 1997), p. ix.

3. Ibid., p. 127.

4. *The American Presidents*, "The Heroic Posture" episode, co-production of Kunhardt Productions and Thirteen/WNET, Kunhardt Productions, first broadcast on PBS network, 2000.

5. William S. McFeely, *Grant: A Biography* (New York: W.W. Norton & Company, 1981), p. 425.

6. Personal interview with John Y. Simon, February 14, 2002.

7. Ibid.

8. Ibid.

Further Reading

Archer, Jules. *A House Divided, the Lives of Ulysses S. Grant and Robert E. Lee.* Madison, Wis.: Turtleback Books, 1997.

Bolotin, Norman. *Civil War A to Z: A Young Person's Guide to Over 100 People, Places and Points of Importance.* New York: Dutton Children's Books, 2002.

Gregson, Susan R. *Ulysses S. Grant.* Mankato, Minn.: Capstone Press, Inc., 2002.

Marrin, Albert. *Unconditional Surrender: U.S. Grant and the Civil War.* New York: Atheneum Books for Young Readers, 1994.

O'Shei, Tim. *Ulysses S. Grant: Military Leader and President.* Broomall, Penn.: Chelsea House Publishers, 2000.

Silverman, Jerry and Susan Swan. *Songs and Stories of the Civil War.* Brookfield, Conn.: Millbrook Press, Inc., 2002.

Spaeth, Frank. *Reconstruction.* Farmington Hills, Mich.: Gale Group, 2002.

Welsbacher, Anne. *Ulysses S. Grant.* Minneapolis, Minn.: ABDO Publishing Company, 2001.

Internet Addresses

The History Place: The U.S. Civil War 1861–1865
<http://www.historyplace.com/civilwar/index.html>

The Ulysses S. Grant Association
<http://www.lib.siu.edu/projects/usgrant/>

Ulysses S. Grant Home Page
<http://www.mscomm.com/~ulysses>

Ulysses S. Grant Network
<http://www.css.edu/usgrant/>

Places to Visit

Illinois

Ulysses S. Grant Home State Historic Site, Galena. (815) 777-0248. This is the house Grant was given by the people of Galena after returning from the Civil War. Open year-round.

Mississippi

Vicksburg National Military Park, Vicksburg. (601) 636-0583. A driving tour; a visitor center museum; the recovered USS *Cairo* sunk during the war, and Vicksburg National Cemetery offers insight into the siege led by Grant. Open year-round.

Missouri

Ulysses S. Grant National Historic Site, St. Louis. (314) 842-1867. The focal point of the national historic site is White Haven, the Dent family plantation. Gravois Creek, which Grant boldly crossed, still flows in front of the grounds. Open year-round.

Grant's Farm, St. Louis. (314) 843-1700. The Grants' cabin, Hardscrabble, is on the grounds of this wildlife park operated by Anheuser-Busch, Inc. Open year-round.

New York

General Grant National Memorial, New York City. (212) 666-1640. On the outskirts of Harlem is the tomb of Grant and his wife. A small museum is on the grounds. Open year-round.

Grant Cottage State Historic Site, Wilton. (518) 587-8277. The cottage where Grant spent his last days and finished his

Places to Visit

memoirs looks almost exactly as it did the day he died. Open Memorial Day through mid-October.

Ohio

Grant's Birthplace, Point Pleasant. (513) 553-4911. This is the little cabin where Grant was born and lived as an infant. Open mid-spring through mid-fall.

U.S. Grant Boyhood Home, Georgetown. (513) 378-4222. The white brick house where Grant spent his boyhood is furnished with family belongings and personal items. A driving tour takes visitors past Grant's schoolhouse, also open to the public, and other buildings with connections to Grant's youth. Open year-round.

Tennessee

Chickamauga and Chattanooga National Military Park, Chattanooga. (706) 866-9241. A superb visitor center museum and a house used as a field hospital are major draws, but many come for the view from Point Park atop Lookout Mountain. Open year-round.

Fort Donelson National Battlefield, Dover. (615) 232-5706. The fort, a hotel where the Confederates officially surrendered, a driving tour, and a national cemetery can be visited here. Open year-round.

Shiloh National Military Park, Shiloh. (731) 689-5275. A visitor center museum and a ten-mile-long auto tour with wayside markers commemorate the bloody battle. Open year-round.

Virginia

Appomattox Court House National Historical Park, Appomattox. (804) 352-8987. The McLean House where Lee surrendered to Grant is the focal point of this recreated Civil War-era village of twenty-seven historic buildings. Open year-round.

Petersburg National Battlefield, Petersburg. (804) 732-3531. Visitors can still see remnants of the famous crater, along with a sixteen-mile-long driving tour and an audio-visual map display in the visitor center. Open year-round.

Index

A
Adams, Francis, 70
Adams, John Quincy, 111
Ammen, David, 59
Appomattox Court House, 44, 47
Arthur, Chester A., 99

B
Babcock, Orville E., 60, 64, 87, 88, 110
Battle of Chattanooga, 43
Belknap, Amanda, 89, 90
Belknap, William W., 89, 90, 91
Blaine, James G., 97
Boggs, Louise, 32
Booth, John Wilkes, 47
Bragg, Braxton, 43
Bristow, Benjamin H., 78, 86, 87, 88
Buckner, Simon Bolivar, 38

C
Camp Salubrity, 22, 24
Chang, Li Hung, 96
Chase, Salmon P., 70
Civil Rights Act of 1875, 84, 110
Civil War, 5, 36, 49, 67, 78, 101
Clymer, Heister, 90, 91
Colfax, Schuyler, 56, 57, 73
Confederate Army of Northern Virginia, 42
Confederate States of America, 5, 36
Corbin, Abel, 60, 62
Cowell, John, 95
Credit Mobilier, 74

D
Dent, Fred, 20
Drexel, Joseph, 103

E
Enforcement Acts, 65

F
Fish, Hamilton, 60, 67, 68, 79
Fisk, James, 60, 62, 110

Fort Henry, 37
Fort Sill, 90

G
Garfield, James A., 97, 99
General Grant National Memorial, 106
Gettysburg, Pennsylvania, 42
Gould, Jay, 60, 62, 110
Grant, Ellen "Nellie" Wrenshall, 31, 80
Grant, Frederick Dent, 29
Grant, Hannah Simpson, 11, 12, 16
Grant, Jesse, 10-11, 12, 13, 15, 16, 17, 32, 40
Grant, Jesse Root, 32, 94, 95, 96
Grant, Julia Dent, 22, 23, 24, 26, 27, 29, 30, 31, 32, 47, 69, 80, 83, 84, 93, 94, 95, 96, 97
Grant, Ulysses "Buck" S., Jr., 30, 99, 100
Grant & Ward, 100-101
Greeley, Horace, 70, 71, 73, 74, 75
Griffith, R. McKinstry, 18

H
Halleck, Henry W., 37, 38, 39
Hamer, Thomas, 17
Harding, Warren G., 107
Hayes, Rutherford B., 93, 97
House of Representatives, 55, 82, 90, 91

I
Indian Territory, 89, 90
Indiana, 94
Inflation Bill, 80

J
Jay Cooke & Company, 78
Jefferson, Thomas, 93
Johnson, Andrew, 48, 49, 50, 51, 53, 54, 55, 56, 66
Johnston, Albert Sidney, 38
Johnston, Joseph E., 49

Ulysses S. Grant

K
Ku Klux Klan, 51, 54, 60, 65, 88, 110
Ku Klux Klan Act, 66, 108

L
Lee, Robert E., 27, 42, 44, 46, 49
Liberal Republicans, 71, 73
Lincoln, Abraham, 35, 39, 42, 43, 47, 48, 50, 53
Lincoln, Mary Todd, 44, 47

M
Marsh, Caleb, 89-90, 91
McClellan, George, 39-40
McDonald, John, 86, 87
McLean, Wilmer, 44
Meade, George, 42
Mexican Southern Railroad, 97, 99
Mexican War, 29, 46, 97
Mississippi River, 5, 7, 8, 32, 43
Mount McGregor, 103

N
New York Stock Exchange, 62
New York Tribune, 57, 70
Northern Pacific Railway, 78

O
Our American Cousin, 47

P
Panic of 1873, 78
Polk, James K., 25, 27

Q
Queen Victoria, 94, 95

R
Radical Republicans, 50, 51, 53, 54, 71
Reagan, Ronald, 93
Reconstruction, 50, 88, 108, 110
Resumption of Specie Act, 84
Richardson, William A., 76, 78
Rosecrans, William S., 43

S
Sanborn, John D., 76
Sartoris, Algernon, 80
Scott, Winfield, 27, 29
Seymour, Horatio, 56

Sherman, William Tecumseh, 39, 43, 49
Simpson, Anne, 12
Stanton, Edwin M., 54, 55
Stevens, Thaddeus, 53
Sumner, Charles, 64, 65, 68

T
Taylor, Zachary, 25, 26, 27
Tenure of Office Act, 54, 56
Thornton, Edward, 68
Treaty of Washington, 68
Trescot, William H., 99
Truman, Harry, 93
Twain, Mark, 101

U
U.S. Grant Homestead Foundation, 15
Union Army of the Potomac, 42
United States Congress, 25, 51, 53, 54, 56, 65, 66, 74, 75, 76, 79, 80, 82, 84, 99
United States Constitution, 55, 66
United States Internal Revenue Service Bureau, 86
United States Military Academy, 17
United States Senate, 54, 55, 65, 68, 91
United States Supreme Court, 108
United States Treasury, 62, 84, 110

V
Vanderbilt, William H., 100
Vicksburg, Mississippi, 7, 42
Virginius, 79, 110

W
War Department, 90
Ward, Ferdinand, 100, 101
Washburne, Elihu, 36, 59
Washington, George, 53
West Point, New York, 17, 18, 19, 20, 36
Whiskey Ring, 87, 88, 89
Wilson, Henry, 73

Y
Yates, Richard, 36